MUSINGS I
SLOUCHING TOWARDS WOMANHOOD
by Patricia Wilson

PUBLISHING INFO
Toronto, Copyright June 2019
ISBN: 9781095973387

Reproduction rights may be obtained by contacting:
godsavethedragqueen@yahoo.com

SPECIAL THANKS
special thanks to Sky Gilbert, University of Guelph,
Hélène Ducharme, Drew Rowsome, Raymond Helkio,
Stewart Borden, Judith Thompson, RM Vaughan,
The Ontario Arts Council, Coach House Books,
Tightrope Books, and Buddies In Bad Times Theatre

CONTENTS

MUSINGS FROM THE BUNKER 2015/17

7

SLOUCHING TOWARDS WOMANHOOD
stories & poems

143

MUSINGS FROM THE BUNKER 2017/19

253

INTRODUCTION
Musings From the Bunker &
Slouching Towards Womanhood

I called Patricia one day about a small edit that I had a question about. We quickly got off topic and she asked me how my day had been going. I told her I had walked up to Seduction, the big sex paraphernalia shop on Yonge Street to buy a strap-on before they closed. I wanted a souvenir from this landmark Toronto sex emporium before it was gone from the neighbourhood. I elaborated a little about my happily realized conundrum regarding the ways in which both femininity and masculinity play themselves out on my body, both sexually and emotionally, and how there was a time when I briefly considered surgery, but ultimately decided that I wanted to keep my penis. I told her that my newly purchased dildo with harness was hollow, and she suggested, jokingly, that I put water in the hollow part and freeze it. A novelty cocktail shaker perhaps, one big chunk to chill the martinis? I then wryly asked her where my member would go if the cavity was filled with ice. Patricia responded to my conversational trans-meditation regarding the positioning of my penis within my amorphous lexicon of gender queer status by saying, "Oh, right, I forgot you have a dick." I was flattered, to say the least.

Before we hung up I remembered that I had called for another reason. I wanted her to send me a photo of the scissors used during her surgery, the ones she describes in one of her many musings, as part of the second section of this book, entitled *Slouching Towards Womanhood*. Patricia's love for Joan Didion and our mutual love for the poetry of Yeats seems a fitting title for the second part of this collection. Didion's famous intertextual citation to Yeats in one of her many acclaimed texts, coupled with Yeats dark and dream-like journey in *The Second Coming* come together in Patricia's overall rubric around daily musings that entertain, enlighten, and bring insightful comfort to her many social media followers. In *Slouching Towards Womanhood* her musings frequently take on a poetic form that flirts with the notions Yeats speaks of in his prophetic poem. As a poet, rockstar, queer community icon, and a daily harbinger of nourishing words, Patricia writes with a diverse quotidian impulse that playwright Judith Thompson responds to when she says of Patricia's daily Facebook musings - *"Reading your posts - like reading Proust, but here, and now."*

David Bateman (editor), March 2019

When a vast image out of Spiritus Mundi
Troubles my sight: somewhere in sands of the desert
A shape with lion body and the head of a man,
A gaze blank and pitiless as the sun,
Is moving its slow thighs, while all about it
Reel shadows of the indignant desert birds.
The darkness drops again; but now I know
That twenty centuries of stony sleep
Were vexed to nightmare by a rocking cradle,
And what rough beast, its hour come round at last,
Slouches towards Bethlehem to be born?

William Butler Yeats, The Second Coming

MUSINGS FROM THE BUNKER 2015/17

OCTOBER

Oct 20
A poem woke me up, nudged me in the ribs to get it down. I gave it what it needs to grow later like my own little child. Awake now, the stress of the day has left my muscles and organs sore and twitching. So many small victories won today. Saw the power of the vote empower usually non-empowered people.

The look of satisfaction on their faces and the new light in their eyes may change their whole perspective. Yet too, my own struggle to survive at times takes it toll. Bunker's asleep and there is snoring rolling around the bedroom. Hard to place it but it is like a soft soothing caress to me right now.

Fear is dogging me in this pregnant moment and I may have to flip the TV on to work it out. My eyes tired from trying to write in the dark so sleep may come again soon.

Tomorrow I imagine will be a lighthearted day around me as things were accomplished by so many for so many.

My tools tomorrow will be as much silence as possible with real listening wrapped up and carried with me in a white handkerchief of contemplation.

Have a good one be true and today share the kindness. Today as I was clearing up the desk where all the papers, unmarked CD's and DVDs, beads from broken Kelly Perras bracelets, books by Patti Smith, Eileen Myles, RM Vaughn and Virgin Mary candles, and just piles of assorted cards and shit all accumulated under the now gone computer monitor and hardware, I found a precious gift.

My mother God rest her soul loved writing letters. I still have some and I reread them and the cards she sent over the years, they always make me smile always make me miss her, always make me shake my head as they mark a moment in my life that I had shared with her.

My mother knew how crazy I was about reading, she knew I read nonstop and often over the phone asked about what I was exploring on the page that day.

Well her little nod to me as she loved me dearly but understood very little of who I had become after the years of internal strife and some of my resolutions and my revolutions, her nod her gift was always a little bookmark sent by mail. She searched them out in her travels and sent me ones that had sayings on them that touched her heart. Mom would then write a little note below the saying or on the back as to why it touched her and why she thought of me. Then sign it, Love Mom, or if it was playful she signed it Love Your Mother.

I have lost many of these but still have a couple and I cherish each one. I found a gem of a one in amongst the mess I was cleaning up. Obviously her reward to me for cleaning up my mess. Life can be kind.

Oct 25
two things.

one

I dontunderstandsomefuckingpeople

two

although the bunker is full of life and love with Hélène and the two dogs in the mix I miss having a cat. I love cats but currently it is not a good time for one financially or emotionally. I am at that point where I would love a kitten but the fucking thing would probably outlive me and I would feel bad for all concerned if that happened. Soon perhaps an older perfect fit for our family...When the time is right it will happen.

Sunday. Rest and thank you to Glenn for doing my shift today, I woke up exhausted. My coffee has never tasted so good.

NOVEMBER

Nov 15

A message to my home city Windsor Ontario. If you're missing some talented and really nice people, they're living and loving here in Toronto. I met them and they met each other last night at Buddies over drinks and dancing and good cheer. Thanks to them for taking on Toronto and thanks to Windsor for sending us the ones with good manners. Cheers.

Nov 16

Coffee is going down beautifully. We are eating scrambled eggs and left over Bavette steak. Both four footers are eyeing us as they pretend to not care what we are doing or eating. Of course there is plate licking and pieces of steaks awaiting them as they truly know in their dog minds. Our one splurge in the bunker is fulfilling my love of white daisies. If at all possible we always have a small bunch in front of the window. Woke up to a fresh bunch that Hélène brought home from her dog walk. We are mindfully aware here right now of how powerful love is and we are grateful for that seed of knowledge.

Nov 17

Absolutely no thoughts for paper today. So just reading, among other finds to read, I found some Thomas Merton. Here are a couple of his quotes.

"Art enables us to find ourselves and lose ourselves at the same time."

"The biggest human temptation is to settle for too little."

"Happiness is not a matter of intensity but of balance, order, rhythm and harmony."

Nov 18

Fell asleep before 2am after rehearsals for Thursday's gallery acoustic show. It's been a while since rehearsing in two stretches with a brunch break then dinner break and to learn two new songs in a style I rarely play with. So I will admit to a tad bit of exhaustion from the music, and the contributing weariness which is also entertained by the resulting left over fairly continuous bar tendering stints of last week.

So now I am reading an interesting book on an interesting artist/writer called Conversations with Paul Bowles. Stretching from interviews with various people and publications over his life. Makes me think, as I mentioned to Drew Rowsome the other day, I feel as though I want to write something specifically on what being in my 60s means to me, and therefore those close to me.

For me, my life feels like its wrapped itself around me like a protective cloth with a few spots where too much of one thing or another has slipped under the protection and made me far too aware of the limitations of life and being a simple timed human life.

Anyway, they are shutting the water off here in the bunker from 9am, so art must wait, while I make sure I semi start my day - a shower - coffee pot ready - my little plants in the bunker also need watering. Chores before a full day of paper play, payroll duties etc, and finally a sprint behind the bar for a theatre company's opening night. Have a good one, be kind, if you can't soar to mountain tops, let your spirit soar to its greatest dizzyingly wonderfully creative heights…Be mindful and as free as you can.

Nov 19

Up heading in to work in an hour or so. Show tonight, rocking some of our songs and a Ramones or two. Tired, I let my work seep into my mind space so sleep was a little rough. It happens - part of the day-to-day workings. Waiting for the coffee to finish its journey into the pot. As much as my habit is to make it, everyday it seems I have made it a habit to grind the beans just right, make sure the coffee pot is really clean, make sure the water filter jug is full for the coffee, and then run the machine. At least every other fucking day I forget to put the water in the pot - I do a dry run of just coffee beans. Wtf.

The bunker is completely asleep making noises and dreaming like crazy. Maybe we will see you tonight at the art show we are throwing some songs down for at videofag at 187 Augusta. The notice is somewhere on my page if you're interested 7 to 10 - it's art baby, it's art. Try and be as free as you can, be mindful, and let your struggles of the day inform you not discourage you. Be kind, even in the biggest of tragedies the kindnesses are always noticed felt and make a difference. Just think what our daily kindnesses can do. Cheers!

Nov 19

Reading, writing in my little note book which I know will take much much discipline to get it to type, and I rarely have it these days. Better for me to scrap the notebooks and type directly. My daily morning - two boiled eggs are cooling, one more coffee and in the bottom swing of out the door of the bunker to the world at large. A happy thing, finally after a period of deep sleep the ancestor of one of my mother's African Violets has again flowered. A small delight in a crowded day. Thank you.

Nov 20
Loser I am - played a great gig at video fag but wide awake the old lady is off at 2am ordering Pizza Gigi no matter. I am at Buddies tomorrow afternoon and night. Killing me with delight!

Nov 21

Ahhh i love you Toronto. Hélène picking me up from work at the bar after a wonderful night at the Buddies bar with a long feet-hurting hours event. She agrees to go to A&W with me, it's dinner time for me. We purchase our junk food delight and hail a cab, of course Yonge street is blocked off because of a fucking sink hole on Yonge so the reliable cabs are not to be seen. We get in the cab to go the five blocks and I say to Hélène fuck it smells like crack in here. We travel through the streets with the cab and doesn't the motherfucker stop to pickup a fare with us in the fucking cab. I calmly state what the fuck are you doing? You motherfucker. Calmly as I can be. Get the fuck going two more buildings turn left fucker...he is drooling and mumbling I give ten bucks get out. Only in Toronto.

Nov 22

I still haven't shaken off or changed or reshaped all my youthful hopes and dreams. Oh many have fallen away, some are barely recognizable in the bright light of daylight, and there is perhaps a blurring of purpose, caused by admittedly having seen a few sunrises in my time and quite a few glowing night street lights as well. Growing…

Nov 23

Awake lying here waiting for the sleeping aid to kick in. Early day tomorrow. At the theatre before 9 am. Can't read much as my eyes are too tired. I have the television on between channels of programming so I can have the haunting light in the room, as I strain my ears listening for the clue to some secret awareness around me or buried deep in my muddy consciousness. Sound and the obtuse visions from the light are my wakeful companions. Love lies sleeping beside me, and throughout the bunker. Breathing, dreaming companions aware of self but unaware of my mindful intentions. Soon I will join them, even for a couple hours and we again will share the journey until the day begins.

Till later, hum your hymn of self and freedom, do not fight for freedom outside of you till you have heaved, gnashed your teeth and looked your spirit in the eye and demanded and now understand what your own freedom is. Cheers.

Nov 25

Ok all things aside. Reality is, I asked Hélène to pick me up on her way home and remember we walk everywhere.... deodorant, hand soap, Advil, and something else that slips my mind and she gets all of it walking home at 2am in the downtown in the city of Toronto and what else? Hélène stops at a little crack area store, because she knows I worked all night, as did she, and picks up potato chips and a bonus sour cream for dipping. My Jack and soda and William Blake bio just got tastier. She is the shits. I thank the universe for her every day. And all of you for listening and reading this, life is hard but it's good.

Nov 26

So we left a mic stand in the back of a Beck's cab when we got home from our last gig at videofag. Considered it gone. Nope the cab driver I guess kept coming by my apt building where he dropped us off and asking people if there were any musicians. Looked like he was describing Drew since he called and paid for the cab. Finally through his dispatcher he searched Drew down and returned the mic stand to his place. Amazing. Beck's cab thank you for hiring such a great driver and helping him find the mic stands home. It would have been so simple to take the fuck it attitude and not return it. A good cab story. Drew Rowsome said it was Beck's Cab 709 and to tip him well.

Nov 27

Awake even with the help of sleep aids. Fell asleep for an hour then my legs had painful minds of their own. They have to move or they ache. This is indeed something annoyingly curiously fucking new. Even tried sipping some booze but I can't do it anymore after I have already been sleeping. No taste for it. Of course I would love a coffee but the timing is out of whack for that too…God I would love a day off or two to reset my clock and perhaps my psyche. But shit I just had two days off for my weekend although I think sometimes that's the problem. As I get older my time being regulated from the outside sometimes is devastating to me. As I have said, I don't hate my job, I rather enjoy it and the people I work with, but I have always struggled with being free issues. As a younger person I would work somewhere for maybe even five or more years somewhere and get up one morning and call in done. I would regret and suffer the reverberations, homeless, penniless and getting a job in my situation was and probably still is a soul damaging nightmare.

I am not writing enough that I can feel, or playing music for people enough either, but I am in a clouded funk. Not depressed, not really, I just don't feel whole somehow. Well I was never under the impression life was easy. It's fucking hard but it's still a joyous ride with great people and small kindnesses continuously being dropped upon me. Life is also work we must work at it, it's the part of our real work, working through it so we can do that work.

So now what, I will go back to bed and wait for the outcome of the next few hours. All good even if it's a bit shaky at the moment. Tomorrow's tools are -

baby steps towards the day
mindfulness and a side of being thankful for so much of what I have

Be kind, love and ponder what it is to be free truly free for yourself, cheers.

Nov 28

I swear to God every time I actually stop and listen to Hélène practice for her recital this Saturday she amazes me with her voice. So strong and beautiful just like her.

Nov 28

Ahhh the stories I have heard the stories I could tell… but then again….god love us all…right now Hélène the four footers a few shots of Jack and chips and a cocktail and work in less than eight hours….it's not a good life but it's my life. The damage is well deserved and well loved…no regrets …all heart and smiles and love

Nov 28

Had a dream last night that Crackpuppy was on tour and we did better than break even - Ha - someone must have coated my potato chips with LSD. Ha. Coffee then out the door to work the matinee and do other bar shit. But first coffee.

Nov 28

In the shower to slowly get ready to go back to work for queer sonic temple tonight. Just put a chicken in the oven to roast so I have something to eat with my little rice pasta and carrots and french beans.

Going to relax till it's time to go, read a bit, sip one cocktail and breathe. Life is good. Moments are mindful right now and for that I am happy. Maybe see you tonight at the bar so you can suckfuckknockback some liquid sacraments from the altar at the temple. Come by, do it, it's free before midnight - 5 bucks after and two queens tonight. Sapphire Titha-Reign and

Allysin Chaynes you know that can't be anything but fucked up fun. See you in a few hours fuckers...

Nov 29

What a fucking long day yesterday not bad just busy and long. The whole damn week was like that. I seriously do not know how my non bar co-workers put so many dedicated hours in. They just keep going. Well no complaints I have a great job, great people around it, on all levels. Artists, co-workers and patrons I am grateful. Still my fucking feet and knees are a mess, walking around like I am walking on a bed of hot coals. So the only thing to do is before coffee, a Bloody Mary to celebrate the week. Praise the simple tomato and what it can do to vodka - Be true to yourself today, work towards your freedom - one thought, emotion, and action at a time. Be kind. And as Lou Reed said - "don't believe anything you hear and only half of what you see."

Nov 30
Gay Loblaws supplies - dinner - frozen pizza a bottle of wolf blass cabernet sauvignon…wine laughs and four footers…warm bunker under the perfect lighting. A good Sunday for Hélène and I.

Nov 30
Fell asleep for a couple of hours after one am. Awake and active again by 3:30am seems the way I rest - a couple bursts of sleep especially after working the bar on the weekend. So just back to bed after reading my newly acquired William Blake bio. Amazing read, I mean Blake's writing alone can set a mind and soul spinning and set them ablaze, but even his bio just makes him glow in my mind more. Quiet here in the bunker except for snoring and sleep sounds. My tired aches and pains are present enough to push me into a panic attack, so I am breathing and praying for a better direction/distraction. There is not enough true spirituality in the world today, it's been swallowed by the forced reality of the world seeing itself through technology. We as human beings are at a loss to lose ourselves in ourselves. There are just not enough mystical visions in our day to day lives anymore. With that be kind to yourself and others today. Society exists for itself not for the individual and their personal freedom. Explore freedom as an individual trait it is yours alone your freedom is not shared or duplicated by anyone else, think of it like a fingerprint unique to

you. Take some time today be still and silent have a mystical vision.

DECEMBER

Dec 1
Just in the door from work. Sipping a beer and tomato juice with salt and a shot of tequila with a couple drops of tabasco in the glass. Starting my dinner and Hélène's lunch within the hour but first checking you all out on Facebook to see how the world at large is doing, and then a little book reading. Whew. I did not have a long day but I am fucking glad to be home with my slippers on and my cocktails at my elbow. Hope your night is everything you need it to be.

Dec 1
Ok last post if you're lucky before I move away from the mac. I was thinking who some of the bravest people I know are - and there are many and the list is thankfully long as we need brave people to keep the world spinning. But right now as I was thinking of some of the bravest people I know and I wish I was one of them - they are the artists that struggle to do nothing else but their art. To make that move, to take that chance, to have your heart broken and be degraded at times because you are simply an artist. Brave Brave Brave. Thank You for the struggle, your tears of frustration and joy, and for taking that leap of faith in yourself. That is all, moving away from the mac I have alcohol at my fingertips and that is all I am saying - cheers

Dec 2

Ah real life. Hélène comes home from work at 2:30 am. Comes into the bedroom as I am listening to Henry Rollins youtube stuff and she says I thought you were going to bed? Of course I am sipping a Jack and soda and think of saying I woke up with the devil on my back but instead just shrug and smile as she leashes up the four footers for their last walk. She says I bought you a present its on the table. I go out and it's a can of my favourite hairspray that was on sale at shoppers. I am so happy and touched that she thought of me, the emotion was the same as if she bought me a new cottage on my favourite lake. Love her. Just how special is it to be thought of in an obscure moment in a busy drugstore at 2am on a weirdly warm wet december morning. It's a wonder.

Dec 6

Holly Woodlawn - she sat here in the bunker with us, she was in a leather jacket after arriving on the back of a motorcycle and drank tea and told stories and loved our big dog Gordy and there is more but those moments are for us alone. She made a difference to so many. God Bless her. RIP

Dec 8

Been awake an hour. Pretty quiet, Hélène is asleep-talking and singing lying here next to me. Both four footers are twitching like shit, making the bed feel like a 1960s coin operated massage bed in some cheap hotel off the 401 outside of Toronto. Sunrise in 13 minutes which I don't need to know but it's the age of information you don't need but can't get used to not having if it's not available.

Another surprisingly mild day today. I am guilty of truly not wanting to go to work today, I don't feel motivated or ready to take on the day. My brain, body and psyche are still tired from last week. Ah but lucky I can do it and if I score a few extra hours of sleep this week I am sure I will perk up. Today is my busy one so I have to rev it up. Going to make my pot of coffee and read a bit from a few selected books and then get out the door. I almost read the news today but caught that destructive habit in time. Well here I go, have a day of true kindness and mindfulness. Work towards being free even in the moment and grab a minute to be silent, slow shit down and contemplate. Cheers.

Dec 9

I am awake waiting. I fell asleep shortly after Hélène returned to work after lunch. So midnight. And woke up at 3am from a dream of tornados and lost ways. I am 61 the same age as the Bob Dylan song Highway 61 revisited. A song, a weirdly funny song with all the solutions and trials of assorted events taking place on Highway 61. A song for my year so far and God willing the rest of 61. It's been a ride, I am tethered to it all by my constant moments of thought of what does it feel like now to be who I am at 61. I don't look for meaning but for mindful feeling, I feel the difference in my body, sometimes huge differences sometimes subtle little twitches of muscles and organs or perhaps my toes at night get a little colder than in the past. No regrets just wonderment now at each new day thankful for it and overwhelmed by what needs to be done just as I was when I faced a much younger and different me in the morning mirror. For me there is always love and kindness fortunately in my life but always the fear of the known not the unknown surprisingly. I know what can be my undoing at any moment and I respect and acknowledge it. Life is hard but it's meant to be lived from the tears, to the joys to the art to the too cold toes in bed that right now I am thankful for the big warm dog that has stretched himself over.

As I said waiting for my second shift of sleep it seems to be how it goes for me these days. I want to get up and have a coffee and a little nibble of something but I will wait and see what the hour brings to the quiet bedroom. Slow it down today, stretch yourself do something new and unexpected. It leads to freedom and the growth of the soul. Love is the answer. Cheers.

Dec 9
Been home since around 6pm did very little at buddies work today. Lots of shit here, fucked up my prescription as usual never noticed that there were only so many repeats on it. Hélène grabbed the last box went to the druggist and essentially said - she did it again, can you fix this - after I spent a half hour talking to someone at Rexall and getting nowhere. They - with Hélène -got it done. Whew. been taking this shit since I was like 18 maybe not good without it. Tried to do online banking fucked up my password although I use it almost everyday, so it shut down. Went to the bank got my cash but goddammit I am not good with passwords and renewals and life like that in general.

Hélène had a root canal yesterday but this morning woke with an eye swollen shut and a prizefighter swollen face. Dentist helped her out, but it is soft food for her tonight. She asked for my wild mushroom Orzo pasta tonight so it's sitting there waiting for the girl. Got two hours playing/practicing in on the guitar tonight like a drug almost high from it. Speaking of drugs sipping a fine tequila and a 1664 kronenbourg beer before I kick into dinner. Fuck life is full. Cheers have a great night. PEACE!

Dec 11

Great night. Worked Thom Allison's show he was fantastic. I was glued in one spot in awe. Love him and Micah Barnes so much. Staff at Buddies were shining examples of coworkers and Hélène came by at midnight as I was getting off work and we headed out and grabbed a couple of falafels to take home. Great night now watching the rerun of Raptors ball game tonight. (Hélène loves basketball) Sipping a beer, excited for a project I am starting, life is good. At work tomorrow for 1pm. Have a good night and a great morning slow it all down look at it all in slow motion see what the possibilities are as you breathe it all in. Trust in yourself never doubt what's in your heart.

Dec 12

Climbed out of the fog surprisingly quickly over an hour ago. First shift of sleep done. Slowly walked around the super quiet bunker making my camomile tea which I drink in an ancient hand made tea cup bought by myself over 30 years ago at an art gallery. The cup is for my morning tea only. Dropped two Advils as my back feels as if it is tightening up and too many work days ahead for that. Woke up from soft pleasant dreams which I have lost to my morning routine but I still have their aroma of softness around me. Reading a few tender passages in the Blake bio and re-reading a few pages in M Train. Really quite chilly in here. I am sitting with my hoodie on with the hood over my head for warmth. Won't turn the heat on and take a chance of losing the sleep temperature.

Sadly, my daisies are on their last day but I saw a beautiful bunch at the T market on the way home tied with a red ribbon for Christmas. Well a bit more reading another tea and back to bed. Explore your day as if you were mapping out a new routine, explore new options for yourself within your day. Kindness and mindfulness are my favourite tools for today.

Dec 15
Awake! Awoke to melancholy
a: depression of spirits : dejection
b: a pensive mood
Other forms: plural mel·an·chol·ies

The struggle to be fully human and personally free, in a world of rules, governments, banks and the day to day struggle for the legal tender. Yes it's true as a fully functioning soul or being, it is possible to go between heaven and hell within minutes. We move on. We pray our personal prayers, we fight the melancholy with tenderness to ourselves, to others, to our loves. I surround myself with favourite things, daisies, photos, incense, for quick adjustments. I search for new favourite small intimate things to add to my soul, my well- being chest, so I can touch them, see them and reflect on them which makes me smile and sometimes turns the melancholy to a wonderful heart melody. Cheers. It's either a couple hours nap or coffee - see where it lands. Be kind, contemplate and be mindful as you breathe.

Dec 16

Getting up - a fairly good sleep last night, I don't really remember what feeling refreshed in the morning feels like but after over six pretty well consecutive hours this might be it. I had to plan my sleep time but it worked last night. Of course the next four days are late working nights so I will have to adjust, both mentally and physically. Quiet as usual at this time in the bunker. Reaching over to grab my morning coffee and book to read. I hate finishing books that I loved reading like saying goodbye to someone you shared intimate details with, your confidante. I guess that's why I re-read so many of them. Like my loves and friends dead or alive I cannot totally leave them out of my life even if it's just memories and/or quotes that stay with me.

Start of a long run of late nights it will be a challenge to eat right, drink lots of water and to maintain mindfulness and peace and freedom through it all. Part of our daily challenges to not be lost from ourselves. Well coffee is calling, candles and incense to light, reading to do. Today my tools will be living in the moment and kindness while being surrounded by the chaos of this particular day. As well, focusing on being free within a day filled with others needs and expectations. Not to lose myself to the hive of others dreams and expectations.

Contemplation is the toolbox for my daily work tools. Be kind, love is the answer, slow yourself down even for five minutes and breathe. Cheers.

Dec 18

Blank dreams and body exhaustion pushed me into an early morning consciousness. Up enjoying my coffee while the bunker around me still sleeps. The two four footers are with my favourite two footer as she also sleeps on what we once thought was a huge bed. Of course bed size is proportional to pet numbers and pet size.

Great night last night - the Sheraton Critiques are an amazing thing to watch if only for the excitement of the kids from the performers to those in the audience. A lot of talent in so many areas and ways. Next week is Christmas week, it came so fast and almost unexpectedly for me. I enjoy Christmas for all the kindnesses it brings forth that normally gets lost in the day to day flash and struggle of our human existence.

Hair day today, I am looking forward to my visit with Mikah Styles, we can explore it all through each other's eyes and drink no name lemonade and good strong coffee while he does my hair. Not wishing my life away but looking forward to my day off on Monday.

Well, I have jabbered almost incoherently here long enough, so going to turn things up a notch and head towards my day. Thinking about my favourite quote that I attribute to William Burroughs "love is the answer" - it frames these times well and it is something that must be realized and put into practice. Today stay mindful, find your freedom where you can without stepping on others sense of freedom. Be kind, love your moments and PEACE.

Dec 21

Worked a great shift, finishing off Sharron Matthews and George Masswohl Christmas sing along in the chamber and the hilarious show called drag in a bag in the cabaret. Fell asleep in my chair for 40 minutes, now to send myself to bed - a beer and tomato juice and a sipping shot of very nice tequila. Cheers see you on the other side.

Dec 21

Slow moving day, coffee and breakfast done along with my shower and the tiny bit of paperwork and some phone calls necessary for the theatre. Sitting here sipping a tequila, day dreaming about lottery wins, books to write, poetry to recite, music to create and play, Hélène's wonderfulness, painting the apartment, and the rain and that little bird I hear out my open window over the blowing bedroom fan.

Total daydreaming and that feels like it will be the only true accomplishment of the next 24 hours. Within my walking and wakeful dreams my soul chases and catches who I really am. I get to see what's truly important to me and at the same time I get to rest my being from the onslaught of what sometimes is a very hard existence as a growing human being.

I will admit sometimes a shot or two of tequila can help drop the needle on the daydream and start it spinning and playing. That's my ramble right now, nothing,

nothing, happening and nothing happening is perfect and all I can handle right this minute. Going to have a lie down and rest. See you on the other side. Dream it so you know it when it comes to you. Cheers

Dec 22
Up at 4:30am pushed into wakefulness by dreams and the half conscious thought that it was three hours later than it really was. Now the bunker and its inhabitants are slowly and some vocally fighting the fact that the day must start far earlier than we are used to.

I just got mentioned in a comment about being the cause of sleep ending light in the bedroom, although I was in the other room. Ha.

I have had my pre-coffee snack of raw carrots and brown rice and olive oil sauteed leeks, just finishing reading and drinking my last coffee before the day starts outside in the shining light of day. A bit stunned at all that is running through my mind, I swear sometimes I can live my whole life in a bite of food.

Time to move into the struggle for the legal tender and all that is given to me in a day. Stay calm, and mindful, be kind and again breathe drink lots of water and be your own freedom fighter. Peace.

Dec 22
So since I started my day at 4:30am and after almost eight fucking hours of Red Cross first aid training and a beer and a tequila I only had enough energy to help Hélène make the first of two batches of tourtière. The filling is delicious, I snacked on it so much it became

my dinner…In bed, sleep mask at the ready, good night and bless you all.

Dec 23

Lights on incense lit coffee brewing by 7am today. Six hours of pure sleep. Woke up to dense fog off the bunker balcony so white that the lights on the balcony reflected back into the window and their shining glory seemed to make no flash beyond the small space they, the lights, inhabit.

Feel tired today and am thankful for the day off that I requested and received, as I am behind in a number of things related to this time of year. Read many things this morning but I opened my thick volume of The Outlaw Bible of American poetry to grab a few thoughts, and wonderment, this morning, one of rest and silence. I have read and re-read this "bible" many times over many years throwing it open and exploring the words of the poets randomly or even occasionally searching for an Acker, or a Whitman, a Myles, or even a Ginsberg. Today as I randomly spun the pages I came across an old train ticket bookmarking a page, but it was the ticket that caught me not the passage on the page but the passage the ticket chronicled. I picked it up, a first class ticket from Windsor to Toronto.

A year or slightly more before my mother pulled up her roots and moved to London Ontario to be closer to her young grandkids. She died there, a sometimes horribly painful death at times, but she did not die alone and was not bitter about her circumstances, and was as usual, surrounded by love and family, and ultimately dying not long after moving to her new home. I remember she bought me the first class ticket home as she knew of my anxiety attacks and that I enjoyed a drink and reading while travelling. We always cried when we said goodbye even though during my visits we could go from hand holding, sitting next to each other on the couch, to growling opinions, thrown back and forth between us. I remember on the way home that I couldn't imagine her dying and in that moment as the train picked up speed passing through belle river I believed she would never die. It had to be impossible. So this morning a memory a few tears a lot of wonderful smiles and a realization that love changes, it adjusts, and it can never be harnessed or defined, but it never dies. So that's it for now, love all you can, and have the determination to live the life you were born to live. Be kind. Cheers.

Dec 25

Right now Hélène is singing Christmas carols along with the CD and making her famous cranberry dish as she sips a mimosa in the kitchen. Christmas heaven.

Dec 25

So Merry Christmas to all from all of us here in the bunker. We love this time of year for its softening of the sharp edges that develop around what sometimes can be a hard day to day existence. People are working a little more mindfully towards kindnesses and sharing their love and parts of themselves that are hidden away until now not unlike some secret wonderfully wrapped Christmas present under the tree of life.

We were at a joyfully nice get together last night here in our building and the different people and their love and respect and drunkenness created a train of thought for Hélène this morning. Hélène is a very spiritual person, in fact we ended up together 22 years ago over our hours of talk of the soul and its workings. Hélène is a holy person who like the archangel Michael wields a sword of love and good and wonderment through her sword-like, Godgiven singing voice, that voice cuts through so much shit and just is pure love of life and being human and it brings the spiritual right into the room. She is amazing. Her and I have a different approach to the soul, and search out different spiritual writings, essays, and even tapes and what have you.

Me, I have a fucking degree in philosophy so I tend to read Plotinus. I at that time also studied Zen Buddhism, and later I drew inspirations from the workings of my soul from poets and writers, such as William Blake,

Whitman, Lawrence, Plath, etc and an endless list which grows everyday. I won't mention Hélène's studies as they are personal to her and for her to share.

My point, this morning she was filled with that light that seeped through my sleep mask and woke me up and this was what she shared with me (amongst other things as she followed me to the coffee machine) - "we should celebrate Santa" - the feeling around Santa at this time is one of giving and kindnesses, we shouldn't celebrate tragedy, even if its 2,000 years old, Christ's life was a tragedy, even he would celebrate the feeling of Santa and what it does for so many. Born into tragedy and thoughts of what Christ had to endure in his life does not leave us uplifted. Santa leaves us uplifted and gives us the energy and love to move joyfully today and towards the rest of the year. She said celebrate the joy (Santa) not the tragedy (Christ).

I think Christ would have spent last night smiling as he wrapped gifts for under the tree and turned water into egg nod for everybody. Feel the joy. Hélène fucking rocks. I learn something from her every fucking day. Cheers!

Dec 26

Boxing day delight! Making Mom's Mac and Cheese. Some cocktails and whatever, with Hélène, another good day in the holiday universe in the bunker. Cheers!

Dec 26

Just out of the shower getting ready. Hélène left the joint to do some laundry downstairs. While she was gone I poured myself a beer a tomato juice and a tequila, knowing that considering the day and night ahead of me, and perhaps the one that was left behind me, I should perhaps maybe just take the beer, if that. So when she just now walked in the bedroom, I said a little sheepishly, "I just poured a beer, (pause) and a tequila." She walks by me then stops and turns and looks at me and smiles and without missing a beat she says "Well you can't change a leopard's spots."

Fucking Hell right...

Dec 28

I don't see why there should be a point where everyone decides you're too old. I'm not too old, and until I decide I'm too old I'll never be too fucking old…

That was a great time, the summer of '71 - I can't remember it, but I'll never forget it.

    Lemmy

My heart is broken…lost another hero…more importantly lost a wonderful and true human being who gave it all right to the end. RIP Lemmy xo

Dec 30

At the office early, fridges to be re-built and things to get ready for New Years Eve. And fuck it's going to be great.

A couple gigs of hoop and silk artists and things and a stellar performance from Fay Slift and her dancers/artists, and excitingly 500 or so dancing fools with two DJ's to accommodate. DJ Regina The Gentlelady and DJ John Caffery. It's only 10 bucks and pre-sale tickets at that price are running out the fucking door. Please don't miss out I really want my regulars/friends there to celebrate with me/us this year. A new year coming up not sure what to say about that right now, except Happy New Year and let's see what comes of it. Lets make it a kind, true year for all of us and those around us. Cheers.

JANUARY

Jan 1

New Years Eve at Buddies rocked just ask anyone who was there. Sorry you missed it. Well, we all have our fun, that's what we do where ever we are. Happy New Year may it be all you need. xoxo

Jan 1

So right now this tastes like my best cup of coffee ever, but then again, I say that often. Wandering around from room to room with my thermos full of coffee so it's never over heated but still hot and always at my elbow is the way to go. New Years Day and it is good. Hélène just brought the fourfooters in from a walk and a romp in the snow. We have our black beans simmering on the stove to eat later as a lovely side to some tourtiere. Lots of booze in the house but it's not tempting me today. Yet.

Wonderful, wonderful night at Buddies last night, everything, from the crowd, the performers, our staff, all were stellar and no one lost an eye at the end of it all. So thank you for starting my New Year off with a smile and no stress and only good feelings. I can't wrap my brain around 2016 yet, my expectations and thoughts of the upcoming year aren't forming. I have two little dreams, well, fantasies, I guess. One to own a bunker on a lake or better yet a nice flowing river, where Hélène and our four footers can continue to love each other and enjoy life in the moment, but we must have a couple extra bedrooms for our family and friends to come and hang with us. "Without people you're nothing" JS said that.

The other thing, I would love to create some soul stunning art that I could be happy and proud of. Still neither one of those things or situations are necessary to make me content or happy. Right now this fucking ticking minute I have never been happier. Now that is pretty cool eh! Thanks for your time all of you I am nothing without you all. I hope this year starts out true, with real freedom for you, on the horizon, and most of all I pray for your own personal Peace. Cheers.

Jan 4

Awake for a good two and a half hours already. Tired from exploring the world with friends last night. Our passports were stamped with delight as we travelled lightly but many thousands of miles in our evening together. We started with sparkling France, and immediately arrived for our longest stay in Japan. Here we were taken with the chilled creamy results of what rice can be in a smallish glass and also the wonderfulness of mugs of Japanese hops golden and light. As we almost over stayed our welcome here we had to move quickly although time seemed magically suspended, still, we were growing slightly weary. Moving on we arrived in Mexico, experiencing its shiny tasteful best with a small glass of pure agave savoured appropriately as the sacrament it truly is. Heading home through Tennessee, we found ourselves partaking in the ritual that we here in the bunker all know so well, Jack Daniels followed by his kind sister, pickle juice. Taking leave, with the pickle back family waving good bye to all of us, we, the evenings world travellers, they promised to always keep a light on as a beacon to find our way back to them. We arrived home weary but content. After a night of safe travelling my morning was clearheaded but sleepy. A bit of a day today a few office chores at Buddies but it is essentially my day off so after those chores are done I will escape the bitter cold and hunker down in the bunker with Hélène and our four footers. Stay warm, find your truth where you can, be mindful, and be kind to yourself and to others. Peace.

Jan 5

Heading to Buddies in a bit, working an event tonight so it will be a longish day but not one that I will have any regrets about. Fucking still cold, I know about our Toronto winters and all that it entails but it still hurts at times. Yikes, I am not too old for rock and roll but I guess I am for cold winters. All my morning routines are almost completed and I feel close to ready to take another day on. I looked in the mirror long and hard today and some days the twist and turns of lines and wrinkles on my face declare character and a life well lived. Today all I saw was a lost innocence that was waiting in expectation for something as yet undiscovered. Being human, and living an examined life can lead to astonishing moments of grace and astonishing moments of despair. We spend our lives doing the balancing act between the two, I must always stop and realize that its the work I am doing to get the balance that is more important or just as important than the actual balance itself. There is no answer to being human only the work of being human can be examined and answered. We all do the work on many levels in many ways, we are all equal in that. Well, there you go what the hell was that rant, anyway got to leave the bunker today to do my work so I am done here for now. Stay mindful, kind, and freedom is in your true work. Peace.

Jan 6

Everyone is home, there are yellow tulips in vases in the living room and in the bathroom. I have a cocktail and a book to read in bed before i go to sleep. Right now things are perfect and good enough. Cheers. It takes so little to be happy and fulfilled.

Jan 8

Friday! For all my good intentions today it is 6:53pm and I am still in my fucking pj's. (only my work at Buddies could allow that to happen, I know how lucky I am) I did get lots of writing done and re-typing/editing too. As Hélène was leaving for work she said - "I will get your pills from the drugstore, but get dressed, go downstairs, to the store, move around and get us a couple of winning tickets, a crossword, and a max. While you're down there grab a quart of milk because the other one went bad and make us some mac and cheese for dinner we have everything else here." We have everything else because for things like mac and cheese I always seem to buy double of what the hell we need, but it worked out, I do not have to face a large world outside of the bunker just the little lobby one. Drifting with emotions today back and forth, heaven and hell and back a little of this a little of that. Just another day dancing in the routine. All is good though glad that we are all able to push on into 2016 and there is only 11 weeks till spring. Oh also the bunker is fully loaded with beer, liquor, wine and mix. Well enjoy the rest of your day/night and don't dwell on things you can't change or need to worry about. Stay focused on you and all you are at this ticking minute. Grab your freedom from where you can, be kind and be mindful Cheers Fuckers!

Jan 13

Where accomplishing and realizing your true heart the true dream seems within your grasp all the while the reality and beauty of the mundane escapes and mocks you.

Jan 14

I have been ill since late Saturday including a small fever nothing serious just the fucking flu. I felt better today and went to work for a few small hours to do some ordering and my payroll duties. I felt as though I should return to the bunker and slowly after my arrival I again drifted down both physically and emotionally. This is the way of illness and I frustratingly accept this. That being the case after a glass of red wine and some hard loaded codeine cough syrup I retired to have deep healing sleep filled with codeine and slight fever tinged dreams. I just now awoke hazily with the shared emotion of so many of my friends, my loves of the deep losses of late. The loss of iconic heroes and their true life inspiration and for some their very private soul mate. Still in the haze with my eyes closed these words although paraphrased from Patti Smith came to me: "I will be with you always. He is not dead. He has simply awakened from the dream of life." Cheers. love has many sides. Peace to you all in your time of mourning.

Jan 15

Awake and up but after reading for a while decided to again join the rest of the family in the bunker's bed. Lots of sleep noises and rolling around, so it will be a rest rather than a back to sleep for me. Hair day today in an hour or so anyway. Fairly recovered from the flu, four days. Just a bit of a loose cough rolling around here and there. Hopefully, God love them, some snotty nosed stylish happy queer kid doesn't share their fucking germs with me again this weekend. Reading the new Chrissy Hynde bio, now that I am into it a bit it's like reading a long Pretenders song. We both grew up in the same similar decaying city, same drugs, same bands, same revolution. Of course we know her path eventually, still an interesting read. Busy day, a later Buddies start as I have a show tonight to work. Finally caught up almost on my paperwork after the Nov and Dec non stop cabaret/chamber shows. Great fun but a busy time was fucking had by all. Looking forward to my coffee in a bit and I am trying a new baked on premises whole wheat (I did not know they will slice it for you) bread from Gay Loblaws bakery. I always have to have a piece of toast with my coffee. I find it's easier on my still sleepy stomach. By the way our bread on the whole is shit. With that pearl of wisdom I am done. Stay mindful, be joyful when able, when you share true mindful kindness with someone you are both transformed. Be free in the best way when you can. Cheers.

Jan 15

In my steady morning routine, I get to stumble and trip over the smallest pebbles of spirituality. Almost everyday, it happens, they are tiny little pebbles, but it doesn't take much to stub the toe of my psyche.

Jan 18

Woke up from one of my sporadic recurring dreams. I am in a neighbourhood in downtown Detroit at my favourite family owned tiny corner store where they also sell food and the owner who is Korean is telling me this and that, while he occasionally goes to the fridge to partake of his ever growing collection of different codeine cough syrups and pain killers. I am holding a writing pad and a pen and then a big brown vehicle, a Plymouth Fury, pulls up on the side street and he tells me I must go and quickly. As I step out of his little store I realize I am somewhere else that is familiar but unrecognizable to me. I start walking up a hill and I realize I am completely naked on the curb of a street where traffic is getting busier and faster I hail a cab realizing I have no money just my pad and pen and the empty bottom half of a clear lemonade plastic pitcher which I am holding in front of my pussy.

Then I wake up.

Ha. Well there you go.

Jan 19

We grow old with our beloved animals as they age so do we.

Still it's watching them slowly turn white get creaky less attentive because of hearing loss eyesight loss mental slow down that sometimes makes the awareness of the passing of the years more heightened to me by watching my beloved pets age - more than my own aging as my body changes

Jan 20

So I am almost completely In childhood sickness mode. I am not actually sick. Emotionally bewildered yes, but that's a process that happens just like the expected monthly full moon.

No I mean the times when I was in grade school and had the flu or a cold or my pesky chronic appendicitis attacks. Those attacks brought the doctor to my bedside and he would push here and there and take my temperature and ask my mother questions, then pat my hand and say no not yet, you can keep it for now. Then he would retire to the living room as this was his last of the night call and have a whiskey with my dad and mom.

That sickbed surrounded by my favourite get well amulets and charms and sacred liquids. Books, lots of books and magazines, a rosary within reach, a flat glass of ginger ale or a small cup of water, honey, lemon and whiskey if it was the cold or the croup cough. And my best friend right next to my head the radio tuned to cklw the big 8.

I am embedded right this moment literally under sheets and comforters and heavy blankets with books and magazines scattered about the bed. No radio or tv on, just some ginger ale, water pictures of a saint or two and my mothers bookmarks where I can see them. Almost as if that bookmark will conjure mom up to lean over me and put her hand on my head once more and ask me how I am feeling - yes my dreamy sick bed cosy and waiting for a change in my condition. Comforting, as the memory becomes the perfect medicine. Goodnight.

Jan 22

So I am un-friending people I love because I need to continue to love them, but if they support Trump and I have to read their support I may be unable to emotionally work with them. So far all my friends who are supporting Trump seem to be able to use washrooms without question they are not hated for being trans, queer, same sex, black, brown or poor, a single mom, a woman, an artist and the list can go on. Please don't freak because I de-friended you, I did it out of wanting to be friends on a day to day level. To me, to talk of Trump in any positive way is supporting hate and its culture.

Jan 22

So we have had our breakfast and we are watching a documentary on Larry Kramer and I have one eye and one headphone can on my ear watching the Keith Richards netflix doc on the computer. Oh did I mention I am so enjoying my Guinness and shot of tequila as I undertake all of this wonderfulness. Have a great Sunday and breathe deep. Peace.

FEBRUARY

Feb 1

Wednesday and it is my busiest day. I have a management meeting early afternoon and a bar shift later in the evening, with all that goes in between. I barely get time to think between preparing for my midweek weight workout, doing it and getting the fuck out the door. So I light my candle while I take a few minutes to eat quietly and I think or meditate loosely on what's going on with me. Today I only had a few minutes and I may be sacrificing some time to write this but I realize on days like this all I can do is work on being consciously human and love myself and the world around me. Even looking the mischief of a world gone slightly mad right in the eye, I know still "love is the answer." Be kind today to yourself and to those people and living things around you seen and unseen. Breathe deep. Peace.

Feb 2

I am having the best Jack and soda that I have had in a while....

Feb 3

Since Hélène works till 2am there is always a chance I will come to wakefulness when she settles in to watch tv or read for a bit after work. I can't drink myself down anymore it's not what I do these days and there is a fine line between popping a sleeping pill or not. It is past that time and I am wide awake and it's going to be a long fucking day tomorrow. And typing on this damn thing right now is a mistake. Ha! Well have a good one today stay true and be kind. Peace.

Feb 7

Need something to chase the frozen rain blues away and get the blood moving. So listening to this bar band.

Feb 7

Having a few stuttered moments, trying to leave the bunker within the hour or so. This fucking cold/cough is hanging on and its come to sipping coffee and using a puffer to get it all going. Still I can love rock and roll as I hack and have Hélène yell from the other room

"I can't believe you still have that fucking cough so bad."

FYI I have been to the doctor's and she said its what it is and that I will survive. Good to know.

Feb 8

Been up and down for the last two hours. Wide awake then sleepy. Read one of the books I am reading, and stared out the window at the city. Back in bed sore from that persistent fucking cough and slowly getting ready to get up and start the run of the day. Quiet in the bunker sounds of sleep and dreams are all around me. Stayed home yesterday for fear the freezing rain slippery would fuck me up in a fall. Workout and Buddies (the theatre) top my to do list today. Be kind, be as free as you can, breathe deep, and Peace.

Feb 13

I realize now that the longer I live the less I learn about the world and the more I learn about myself.

Feb 16

Listening to Mad Mad World by Tom Cochrane on fucking cassette as we prepare our first meal of the day. So many great songs on it besides the great singles.

Feb 18

I remember this day and memory clearly. Some things stick some things don't. Beautiful day out today. I am extremely tired from work and being on my feet for three solid bar shifts. Still I got up threw my clothes on and walked with Hélène and the dogs to Pet Value on Parliament and Carlton. Just wanted the sun and the semi-warm air around me. Have a good day filled with all that you deserve. Be kind, don't forget to rock and roll. Peace.

Feb 23

Great night last night for meeting old friends and meeting new old friends. Doesn't get better than that.

Feb 25

Dishes and chores done. Showered, housecoat on and got my lucky scarf and bunker cowboy hat on and started the water boiling for tonight's pasta dinner. One eye on the clock another on this and my Guinness and shot of Jack on ice. Looking forward to seeing some of you tonight for Buddies Saturday night club.

Feb 25

For the last three weeks or so I have come here to spend a few moments writing my usual shit but I have spent more time with my finger on the delete button. Not focused…see I just started to delete this stuff too. Things are ok have spent two weeks working Rhubarb theatre festival and have met some extraordinary people and witnessed a great deal of lovely kind personal interaction. That all happening in the middle of the shit show Rhubarb can be, pretty amazing. But I got nothing to give right now so bear with me and this Facebook page as I throw around pictures and images waiting for that perhaps quiet sneaky melancholy to step aside so I can write and work again completely. Enjoy the ride that you're on, spend a few minutes completely free of expectations. For all of our sakes, create an altar for kindness and worship at it. Peace.

Feb 26
Today as I am unusually alone on a Sunday, I am wandering around the bunker lighting candles, then blowing them out and lighting incense in rooms I don't intend to sit in. I am watering flowers and playing music then putting the water can down half way through the job with some plants drowning while others are screaming at me to continue because they are so thirsty. I pour myself a Guinness and a Jack shot and put it on the table and wander away leaving them lonely and unfulfilled of their purpose. I guess what I am saying, today I am like a ghost with no one and no place to haunt. Just floating and flittering around waiting for a purpose. Be kind. Peace.

Feb 27
Hélène is at her voice lesson. I am moving towards my day, which is starting later than I would have liked. So I drink my coffee for the buzz to get into my workout and this is getting my heart going a little faster as it screams from the speakers and rams the adrenaline into my veins and heart to get me into the weights routine. Have a good conscious day, drink lots of water, breathe deep, and be kind. Peace.

MARCH

2 Years Ago

March 2, 2013
So when is my fucking living room not a living room when it's a rehearsal space for Crackpuppy learning one of the bands acoustic songs....so much fun and booze too!

Mar 4

So work tonight. It's been cool at Buddies on Saturdays. Everybody that should be there, they're there. Come by have some cocktails. Lots of videos tonight for your dancing and viewing pleasure. Having a before dinner cocktail while listening to James Cotton kill that harmonica.

Mar 7

Sipping my pre-dinner cocktail. Ribs, soaked in buttery white wine, button mushrooms, and a mixture of parsnips, carrots, and red onions with brown butter. Brown rice with warm chicken broth and butter to top it. Feeling the bunker and all it is tonight. Life is fucking hard but we can do it one moment at a fucking time. Cheers. Breathe deep, and Peace.

Mar 8

Hélène is up for a 7:45am doctors appointment. Needless to say she is not happy and quite crumbly vocal about it. We just had dinner at 12am this morning for fuck sakes. Living our storybook lives under a broken clock.

Mar 12

I re-read this and remember why I wrote this…it seems a good thing to re-share today. Have a day of your truths and be kind.

5 Years Ago - Daylight savings time is like a hit and run. It hits you, then it takes off leaving you with whiplash and a concussion. Bourbon helps.

Mar 21

Home from a short day at the theatre. Paperwork, payroll, and saw someone I really care about that I don't see often. Now down to business - a Guinness and bourbon on ice and I am in the process of making our dinner for Hélène and myself. It's a late one as she is working and my dinner is her lunch but we don't follow the clock all too well here in the bunker anyway. Making spaghetti with cannelloni bean bolognese for the first time and i am thinking it's going to be tasty. Have a good one breathe deep, drink lots of water and fight to be as free as you can. Be kind.

Mar 25

Sitting here reading in my reading corner, just finished my thermos of coffee. Buddies will be exciting tonight with the march of the queens at 10:30 and dj Margot with guest Dj Regina the Gentlelady spinning all night. As the quiet settles in at my feet this is happening, to add to that, I am certain life right now is a grand feeling. Have a good one, if you're around come by at 10:30 to Buddies and watch the show and dance baby dance. Be kind, fight the fight for your freedom, and Peace.

Mar 28

Oh shit even with a sleeping pill I am wide awake. Must have been the excitement of a date night with Hélène, we were guests in an executive box at tonight's Raptors game. It was great, but Hélène was beyond ecstatic (we won handsomely too) so I was happy happy for her. A great time, great people with us. Thanks Brock, it was perfect timing as I mentioned to you. Then we came home and were mouth open astonished at the movie The Black Swan. Holy shit that is all I will say about that. If I was still the old style drinker that I was in the olden days I would be smashed by now trying to drink myself down but alas my soda water with a touch of lemonade for flavour is going to have to take me where it will. Have a great day be free as you can and Peace

Mar 30

Back in bed after a three hour break from sleep. Read a bit, wrote to chase some terrifying demon dreams away. Drank water to quench a sore/soar throat, probably that way from the psyche screams of my dreams. I also worked with our plants watering them, a caress here, a soft word there. Read through pages of a few books, fiction, bios, finally some poetry. At arms reach my go to, Howl by Allen Ginsberg. This is the blanket of words I pulled around me to warm me as I headed back to bed.

"Holy forgiveness! mercy! charity! faith! Holy! Ours! bodies! suffering! magnanimity!
Holy the supernatural extra brilliant intelligent kindness of the soul!"

Allen Ginsberg

APRIL

Apr 1

It's 9:32am and as i go back to bed to catch a bit more sleep, I found this to tuck me into bed.

"In my way of thinking, anything is possible. Life is at the bottom of things and belief at the top, while the creative impulse, dwelling in the centre, informs all."

Patti Smith, M Train

Apr 2

Whew the day has been full and wonderful. Right now a cold Jack and soda at my elbow and it won't be the last but not too many more. Went to work (Buddies in Bad Times Theatre) on my day off. Saw Our Town. Hung and watched the show with Brock Hessel. The show was more for me than I could have imagined. Met Hélène there after and went point shopping at Gay Loblaws and bought supplies for our dinner get together (Mexican fair) with Hugo Rempel and Corser Dupont. That was amazing company and it made the food taste even better. The Bunker is clean and ready for another tomorrow. Behind me Hélène and the four footers are napping loudly and happily. Gibson was so happy to hang with the boys tonight and Marlie loved the extra pats and scratches. Thanks to all for the day… Another Jack and soda and I just had the last shot of dangerously smooth tequila. Good thing i am off tomorrow.

Apr 3

Coffee is going down. Hélène and the four footers are back from their walk and she is making our breakfasts. They get their usual dog food and roasted chicken that I made for them last night and we get a wonderful breakfast burrito. Our days off is today and it was my first usual workout of the week. I don't do maniac shit working out, only free weights for 20-25 mins three sometimes four times a week and the last set to exhaustion. I can't do bootcamp any longer as my poor body has too many creaks and crevices in it. As I say I don't work out to look good I work out just to get up the fucking stairs. For those who are wandering around the earth close to my age of 62 I so recommend something similar to what i do. So little time, so many benefits. Enough, I have breakfast waiting so off I go. Enjoy the day, stay calm, watch for that moment of freedom that you can embrace, always choose kindness and Peace.

Apr 4

Awake. The city from 20 something floors up has disappeared under a thick bank of wet fog. I have crawled back into bed just because the reality of starting a day outside the bunker doesn't seem like the proper reality yet. Soon though. Hélène is sleeping not noiselessly beside me while the four footers are lying around the room and on the bed like quickly discarded dresses. Don't really have a sense of myself yet, but the fog in my head is slowly lifting if not the one outside. Busy day ahead, off to the theatre later for a daily dose of desk work and I have a poem kicking around in me that needs to see the light of day. Well wide awake so time to grind the coffee beans and partake of my first addiction of the day. Embrace your life and create your truth the best you can. Choose kindness and Peace.

Apr 4

Good day, got the payroll done, some paperwork, booked some repairs and ordered the booze, baby. More to do tomorrow but now home and napped. Went to Gay Loblaws and we are having tequila soaked catfish with brown rice and onions and portobello mushrooms and fried cabbage with onion and bacon. Of course went to the liquor store picked up a bottle of Jack Daniels and a bottle of silver tequila which is always a treat to have around. The Jack is necessary and the tequila is the treat. Exhausted when I came home, as I was up before 7am and had gone to bed at 3am so i needed a nap. A dangerous game napping at

7pm when I get home, one minute too long immersed in a nap, and that's it, my night sleep is fucked. You know what they say - a successful career is all about drug management. I got home had a half a shot of tequila to help me get sleepier and I had saved a half cup of coffee from this morning in my thermos which I downed after the shot. Perfect, out in minutes and awake and refreshed 20 minutes or so later from the coffee kicking in. Now writing this as dinner cooks in its stages and I scribble the beginnings of a poem and a short story. Can't wait to see Hélène at 10pm when she gets home for lunch and we can share our food together. Well if you made it this far in my post sorry it's just a boring little rambling with nothing supporting the time it took to read the fucking thing. No magic just a sidewinding rambling like a snake in the desert sand looking for a reason to be in the sun and heat. Peace.

Apr 6

Excellent. Work gig starts earlier today so went to bed before 2am so I can be up and rolling by 8am or 9am. Hélène came home from work at 2:30am and eventually and quietly came to bed. The four footers were settled on the bed and her favourite movie came on. Trouble with the Curve with Clint Eastwood, Amy Adams and Justin Timberlake. A great baseball and relationship movie, I love it too. Even with my earplugs and sleep mask on I could sense her joy at watching the movie and I woke up. So at 4:15 halfway through the movie I surfaced to watch it with her and enjoy her joy. So why do I love her?

Me: Hélène now that I am awake, want to split a beer and have a shot of tequila.

Hélène: Ok, sure, want to have some tortilla chips and cheese too?

The commercial comes on we both jump up, me to pee and then move to the kitchen to get the tequila and her to get the beer and chips and cheese. It's the best, really, absolutely a simple thing that makes life so full. She is now, as are the dogs, sleeping of fucking course, and I am wide awake, but fucking hell I wouldn't want it any other way. I would rather be exhausted today rather than to have missed my 4:30am rendezvous with Hélène and our half of beer and shot of tequila and a few tortilla chips and cheese. Life is hard and it's too fucking short, I don't want to miss out on the real moments. Glad I have coffee in the pantry and it's not work out day. Have a good one, stay focused on the moment, breathe deep, choose kindness always and Peace.

Apr 7

Tried to write something today but this little phrase kept coming into my mind and exhausting me. Fucking Hell. The phrase i created of my own accord was this: "Really? Just because you invoke the name of your god it's then ok to use over 50 tomahawk missiles on a country and even worse, without even consulting anybody in your 'democratic' nation. What a shit show."

Exhausted, heartbroken and feeling a bit doom and gloom. I have said this before but it means more right now Peace.

Apr 8

So steadier today. Up earlyish after a late night bar gig at buddies. Helped Hélène make the breakfast sandwiches after she walked the dogs and she bought them their whole roasted chicken for the next couple of days. Decided to make pasta tonight for dinner for her lunch - my dinner before my club shift. Oh by the way at Buddies, we have Katinka Kature hosting our now every Saturday Queen floorshow from 10:30 to around just after midnight with Dj Regina spinning tonight. It's so fantastic and so different from what we were and yet still the same. Come check it out. Anyway, making pasta involves leaving the bunker to go to the butcher and Gay Loblaw's and Pusateri's grocery store and spend time with what today seemed like 200,000 people. Still made it back safe and sound only slightly shook and dishevelled. Sauce is on now and cooking for a couple hours to eventually cover the Penne with glorious flavour (hopefully). Soon i will have a Guinness before dinner then out the door to start my night/day. Tomorrow starts my weekend, hoping for some rest and time with Hélène and the four footers over the next couple days. Stay true to you even in the face of uneven odds. Be kind first - second, Peace.

Apr 10

Hélène and I went to Gay Loblaws to buy dinner supplies after we had delicious Ramen and came home to rest. I guess I was exhausted. I fell asleep for almost 4 hours while Hélène watched basketball and napped off and on. Couldn't bring myself to make dinner, so for dinner at 12 midnight she scrambled me two eggs with a piece of brown bread toast. She wanted second day pasta. So 3:27am we are having a couple cocktails and about to start our second game of scrabble. Exciting living in the bunker. Have a good one today. Love all the truths in your life, be kind and Peace.

Apr 12

Up for an hour. My now usual two part sleep. 10 or 11pm bed till 2 or 3am then back to bed till early morning. This currently works for me if I do not have a super late event to work. I try and get up between 6am and 8am on workout days so I can get the pre workout coffee in me, work out, and still have some quiet contemplation before I hit my little easy weight routine. Then I have to push the boat away from the dock at the bunker and go fish for our dinner/living. Life starts out in the moment here and if I am not hungover (which is rare these days) I am truly thankful for the life I have been given to me by my parents and all those who I love and those I share every day with. Well time to bribe Gibson into the bedroom with the rest of the family so I can have my workout mat back. Take care live your life fight to be free it will always be a fight and may you know true Peace deep inside and around you.

Apr 14

Good Friday! For me it always seems a little quieter. The ritual is in my DNA. Sitting in my reading chair having a cup or two of coffee before I work out and Gibson's deep sleep breathing brought my eyes to him lying nose to nose with himself in the floor mirror. Have a good one. Close your eyes even for a moment to our shattered world and rejoice that you are who you are. Love as much as you can, be kind first and Peace.

Apr 16
Easter Sunday Toast with olive oil and coffee on the bunker balcony.

Heavenly.

Apr 16
Easter Sunday! Now making a frittata with the left over spaghetti dinner that I made last night. Made another thermos of coffee and Hélène and the four footers are back from the first venture into the neighbourhood. I have what is my favourite go to album on Let It Bleed by The Rolling Stones. Beautiful - a true work of art. And let me say it is on a not too gentle volume. Have a good day, Peace! Peace! Peace!

Apr 17

Hélène just finished potting some herbs that were given to us last week. She is full of the smiles of the possibilities of summer on the balcony. I did my work out as she happily got her hands dirty, as my back was bartender tender when I got up this morning. So of course I waited and worked out later. Today I am swamped with the flashes of moments filled with emotion, and thought, travelling between forever and nowhere and heaven and hell. Not a bad day just one that could go anywhere at any moment. Thinking about all those I know and don't know battling disease and fighting the fight for life and their outstanding bravery and thinking also that I am surprised and thankful I am not among them.

The poet, all things are examined and set reeling into the subconscious and the truths coming back are not always to the liking. Yet a saying which I love does run along as such: "an unexamined life is not worth living" (Plato's Apology, which is a recollection of the speech Socrates gave at his trial.) I am aware that there is a trip to Gay Loblaws in the very near future to get a few supplies for dinner tonight. To make that move out of the bunker with Hélène for a mutual journey of exploring our options will be soothing to the mind and soul. Listening to Lou Reed and enjoying all he has to offer. Well, have a good one, choose kindness and Peace.

Apr 17

Sipping what may be the best Jack and soda I have ever had, well at least today so far, while waiting for Hélène to finish her daily vocalizing. I have some guitar practicing a little later while the NBA television (basketball for those who are not in the know) takes over certain areas of the bunker. Soon hitting the street to get our dinner supplies but right now watching this as the Jack infused ice cubes freeze my tongue and bang off my teeth. Perfect.

Apr 18

Worked out when i got home from work as I had such a fucked up back when the morning came to me I had to wait till the day had strengthened my body and resolve. Now sipping a Jack and soda and watching clips of Frida Kahlo and others who cross my mind. Soon dinner/Hélène's lunch for 10:30pm. Baking a chicken and doing rice and beans Jamaican style with a side of asparagus. My girl loves the rice and peas as she calls them. Glad to make her happy. Have a full night of things you love, let kindness make as many choices as possible in your life. Be free, and Peace.

Apr 23

What a great night last night at Buddies a busy busy Saturday night lovely friends from the past…remember you can never make new old friends so always a pleasure to see those who have memories with you. And fuck - those queens ripped the fuck out of the place last night dancing and moving every inch of space in Buddies. Thank you to Jenna Syde for working the small room bar while Katinka Kature, and then Baby Bel Bel were dancing on the bar behind her in what we call 'queen on the machine' - it was busy baby, it was fun thank you also to Katherine Hytes Dior, and Heroine Marks for great shows, and Dj Regina the Gentlelady for the best music and vibe to match those dancing bitches.

I am celebrating this morning with a cold beer mixed with salt and tomato juice just to take the edge off and to start the day forward.

Apr 25

Morning and the start of the week struggling for enough legal tender. Coffee is close to done and Hélène is getting ready to make us a breakfast burrito. I was thinking of pain and empathy - a left over from conversations last night over dinner with MC and Hélène. We talked of how true empathy makes one person while the lack thereof makes a totally different type of person and how important empathy truly is to us as a community of flawed human beings. How empathy and kindness help us see ourselves within the community and in each other. We see ourselves and recognize ourselves in each other through the many kindnesses and the empathy that we practice and come to know. From there I moved into the thought of pain and the empathy we can have for someone's pain because if we take a moment we again recognize the pain in ourselves. Yet try and describe pain try and tell someone what your pain is like or try and understand the pain being described to you from someone else, it's impossible. Pain escapes language and I remember reading something Virginia Woolf (paraphrasing here) said about pain. "We can describe the words of Hamlet clearly but we cannot describe a headache." So our empathy is felt of course rather than understood through language. It is in our DNA to be recognized or ignored. If it is ignored and empathy is left cold and bruised and dying by the side of a dusty little used road the results are tragic and even devastating to all of us. Ok enough, the day is starting its roaring engines and I am about to leap into it and give what I can where I can. Be kind, explore true empathy and Peace.

Apr 26

Because I got up and was so exhausted this morning for no fucking reason I did not work out on my usual Wed morning. Still, worked today at that crazy fucking theatre which I love but out the door in time to make it to Cumbrae's the butcher to get a tiny little whole chicken to bake for the dogs meal tomorrow and one of their super delicious chicken pies with bacon and snow peas. Three meals each out of that pie, what a deal. I still had coffee in my thermos from this morning so I downed it and when it started vibrating my hormone drenched body I felt, among other things, like working out. Did that, baked the damn chicken for tomorrow, and Gibson the four footer and I shared the chicken legs as an after workout boost. Now baby, the Jack Daniels is swirling around in its home in the special stupidly expensive skull glass and the Stones are on the stereo. Revving me up to jam on my acoustic… Cheers.

Apr 29

So if the apocalypse is to come in a flash and I know that as it overcomes me I will not be praying or asking for forgiveness of sins spent and collected. My reaction will be "Oh fuck" or something like "Jesus Christ, really?" So, because i know we are so close to the end, if things continue as they are guided by ego maniacs bent on making their little dicks look bigger, I want to send out this message to the spirit in the sky;

Forgive me, forgive all of us who have shown what love is, in whatever form it has taken. We have loved and shared kindness in the shadow of a darkness that you allowed to grow. Perhaps it's time for us to go but remember all of us, some like me, a sinner, but a clear headed true humanity lover. Of course I could ask that you, spirit in the sky, you add up the good and the love and the struggles to be all we could be as humankind. Although it's a close game on good and evil when the dust clears after the slide into home plate I think evil will have dropped the ball and good will be safe and win the game. Give us another look. That is all.

MAY

May 3

Still there are still quiet moments when the bunker is asleep in peace. A new book to read, while sitting in my reading chair, and a thermos of coffee at my feet. These are gifts of life and thought. A lit candle and incense for the moment and for all those I love, past and present, of this earth and beyond. Here now there is nothing else.

May 4

Rainy day and looks like a rainy few days. Hélène has walked the dogs and is out doing some personal chores. Myself, finished my coffee and toast and eggs with tomato and about to start the trip towards exiting the bunker and off to the theatre to do some paperwork and work Sky Gilbert's opening of his new play tonight. If you're around Glad Day Bookstore tomorrow (Friday 7pm) Drew Rowsome and myself will be part of this gig there. I may read one of my new poems if time allows. Drop by - it is Steve Keil's poetry book release a really nice piece of the written word and Paul Bellini is giving a reading of his equally astounding work. Peace

May 6

Oh fuck I can't get my shit together today to move at more than a snail's pace. Worked out had a shower started the rice for dinner. Yes I did have enough energy to make the best before dinner/work Jack and soda that I have ever had but my scope of events which included a trip to Gay Loblaws is getting smaller. We will see what the moments bring in the next bit. Have a good night, be safe, be kind. And if possible have a hellaofagoodtime. Peace.

May 7

Sitting quietly in the living room while Hélène not so quietly screams at the Raptors on television. Fully aware that Cleveland and Lebron James are playing better in this series than at anytime in the season. Still after a night of work quiet is my way. To help with the quiet a cold beer and tequila. Cheers!

May 8

The day of life on the run from solitude is slowly beginning. Another cup of coffee a toast and a poached egg for fuel and a few more pages of the book I am reading. Gibson is snoring and twitching in his dream of dreams on the couch beside me and it's a good moment. We brought in from the balcony over a dozen plants from herbs to flowers because of my fear of overnight frost. Barely room to walk around the dining room table. I can't tell if I am aching because I do not feel well or because I added another fourth day a week to working out. Doesn't matter, probably a bit of both. Still, running towards my daylight day to day life. Haven't unpacked my gear from Friday show so it also crowds the space in the bunker, something to attend to tonight. Well, pushing the go button on this machine and making the move. Be kind, work to feel good and as free as you can. Peace

May 9

Home from work easy day except for a few things that were out of my control but it happens. And it will be taken care of easily. That said, a rich Guinness and some Jack on ice on the side washes the shit away and strengthens the good. Going to make dinner a little later as Hélène is at the opera with David Grenier. Had all these things I wanted to do tonight but completely uninspired. So I am going to have another set of cocktails and watch the "The Future Is Unwritten" the documentary on Joe Strummer. That will inspire me on many levels. Have a good night stay calm look to the horizon not for your future but for the light to make your heart and soul glow. Peace.

May 10

I was going to write this piece this morning just after my measured moments were settled in my head on how they would pan out for the day and when and where they would take me. I sadly miscalculated as I normally do, when I have a meeting to be at, and therefore I was behind the eight ball of time running out. So when I got up and slipped my slippers on and moved to the bathroom to drink the hot tap water and wash my face into its morning grin the anxiety of someone else's expectations of my time caused me to become blurred and rushed and I started to miss the small and precious little moments at my fingertips. I could feel our little maybe 15-year old small four footer Marlie between my ankles oh so silently just waiting for me to acknowledge her. As I lowered myself to sit and pee she cozied up against my ankles to be petted, purred at, and complimented on her wonderfulness, beauty, and loyalty, and to remind me of love given. Today as I looked at her she was a little more feeble, a little bit more tired perhaps. She has gotten more needy as the years have whitened and dulled her fur, clouded her eyes and weakened her once nimble and strong limbs, and she now has small little seizures that are becoming more and more common. As I looked into her eyes I am sure I caught her acknowledgement of her mortality. I thought she knows, she knows we are counting down the clock to her not coming out of one of these seizures and our time together is now slipping away from us. Of course sadness overwhelmed me and although I felt the tug of time and meetings, I took a deep breath sitting there on the toilet, and stopped time to just enjoy sitting and petting her for all she was worth and has been for all these years.

Marlie, who was cooing as she accepted my acknowledgement of her. I don't know how to acknowledge all the world that is in my heart. How do I do it face to face before we can't do it face to face. So two things, I will put love first before schedule if I can and acknowledge in my heart every morning all those who fill my life and try and appreciate them while we are still able to be eye to eye, word to word, voice to voice…Well fuck that was a minute. Be kind, don't let a schedule deny you a moment of love whatever kind of love that may be. We were human and love before there were schedules. Peace.

May 12

As I drift off to sleep with a day's and life's works trailing off me like stardust on a passing comet this comes to me - "Every moment has it's story and every story is worth its telling."

May 13

Beautiful day getting ready to leave the office here at Buddies and get some dinner supplies. Sad but true we lost our iMac and I think all that was in it. Back up wasn't backing up…All things on the iPhone now until we can afford a new computer. Oh well can only deal with what I have, not what I have lost. Fucking hell! So things are going to come slower here and I lost my YouTube time for awhile. Ha - new habits will arise out of this. So glad we can feel the summer coming down the path just over the hill from us. Have a good one enjoy the day. Be kind Peace.

May 13

Oh it's going to rain maybe storm but I am home safe and sound with fresh Ontario asparagus and fiddleheads. Yes. Sipping my pre-workout coffee while Gibson does his usual check of the weights and mat to make sure all is safe.

Happy Mother's Day to my Mom, and my Grandmothers who did their bit for love and family and have passed on. I still love you even if I can't look into your eyes while you give me advice, love or shit. Rest in Peace. Happy Mother's Day too to my sister who is the best mom ever she still gives it all and she just continues to grow and give so she can be what it takes to be a mother in these hard fucking times. She is the best. Happy Mother's Day to all mothers today they have the power. I have to say Happy Birthday to all the same sex partnered moms and queer ones and say you astonish me with choosing love over the common sense of easy. We know how hard it is to be queer and you my dears put that in the forefront and said fuck you to all those who would say you shouldn't, mothers babies and children. Bravely mothering children that could help change the very DNA of our human race and society. God Bless all Moms here and beyond. Peace.

May 17

Hmmm had work to do in the cabaret but there was art going on so an excuse to say fuck it and come home and sit on the balcony with Gibson the big 110 four footer whose head is resting on my feet. Oh did I mention I am sipping a tequila, Campari, grapefruit, beer cocktail. Beautiful day a good moment, my moment. Cheers.

May 22

I am sitting in the bunker with brunch almost on the table and a coffee steaming next to me as the live velvet underground record works it's magic. And I was thinking about Pride - the young and old the fresh ones and some like me that are closer to the finish line than I ever expected to be. I thought of those that came before me and fought battles for their truths that I can only imagine. Then I found this quote from one of my favourite authors and it felt right.

"To us, their less tried successors, they appear magnified...pushing out into the unknown in obedience to an inward voice, to an impulse beating in the blood, to a dream of the future. They were wonderful, and it must be owned they were ready for the wonderful." - Joseph Conrad, Lord Jim

Be kind, don't get up in the morning and look into the mirror and see a fucking asshole. Peace!

May 23

Well due to something belonging to Toronto Hydro that is located somewhere in our buildings lower catacombs needing fixing we have no water, hydro or elevator till 2pm. Dogs were walked and relieved early as were we and hard boiled eggs tomatoes and bread are available. Coffee in thermos and tea cozied up. Hunkered down for the time we are going to plant flowers and wait it out. After working on my feet all week twenty-something floors of stairs are not an option. Some things change and adjust as time carries you along. Stairs and over exertion are among those. But my acoustic guitar is ready and I can read and write when not helping Hélène plant. Have a good one we are bunkered down. Peace.

May 25

Rain - lots of it today. Workout happened watching sheets of wind blown rain batter everything on the balcony. Flowers are safe though as window boxes get planted tomorrow. Have a couple chores to do and errands and work of course is lying in wait for me. Can't shape any thoughts about my life today everything is floating by without effect. No revelations coming my way today except at least the attempt at examining my life and its coloured, dented, moments is as good as it gets today. The journey baby it can be as great as the destination. Have a good one be kind leave the assholes you meet in the day and maybe in the mirror behind and move towards a good day. Be free and Peace.

May 26

Fuck I am home from work thank god. The work day was cool people were cool. But shit I was jonesing for the bunker and a large triple Jack and soda. Started the day on the run to make the management meeting - almost was on time and god bless my coworkers for understanding my shitty tardiness. Worked on paper shuffling phone calls had some laughs a great couple of face to face conversations then back at home at 5pm to get my workout in then on the run to make it back to work to open the bar for the youth elders show which on it's fucking preview was sold out.

Fuck they have been working their hearts souls and minds and giving it all. Worth the time to see I think. Now I have that Jack and soda with me as I watch a great DVD of the rolling stones Exile on Main Street tour (1972) brown rice boiling and a roast of peameal bacon which I infused with dijon mustard and good old maple syrup. Fresh asparagus as an added treat. Hélène's lunch and my dinner at 11pm. Thankful for it all and hopeful for another chance to live the life tomorrow. Work on being free and who you really are. Don't be an asshole and be kind. Peace.

JUNE

June 4
Homeonthebalconyinthesunreadingandaguinnessandtequilathatisall. Happy Sunday.

June 4
Tonight!!! It's getting closer to Pride... come out and drink/dance and watch an epic drag show (or 2). I'm bartending the Satellite Bar serving all of the dearest and Queerest! Shooter specials…Kween Go-go dancer's and Pop tart beats!

June 10

Home from the theatre and all that fucking art.

It's cool but sometimes it's about buying groceries for dinner and a sunny day with my four footers and a Guinness and a shot of tequila on the bunker balcony. Peace.

June 11

Holy shit yes I am sick but I am into my second sip of Jack Daniels and soda and I feel way better. Hmmmm I have some sore and bent and badly healed once broken toes and foot that hurt like fuck. Needless to say as I am typing this with one hand I am pouring some Jack Daniels on my fucked up foot. Probably will fix it up just beautifully. Cheers.

June 11

It's hot but a beautiful day. I awoke to a full cold with a sore throat that is killer, Marlie the little four footer has diarrhea and Hélène is away till tomorrow afternoon. Fucking hilarious. But my coworkers pulled up to the gate and I have tonight off to get a little better and to clean up dog poop. Thankful for that. Just barely able to eat an avocado and a tomato but did drink a pot of coffee and sipping on an ice cold fucking light beer (Hélène's). So nice having the balcony flowered, fountained and sunny. Takes all the edge off of an upcoming busy work month. Ahh last night I managed to draw a little baby raccoon trapped for a while in the theatres vent system into the dressing room washroom vent and after I took the cover off it was free in the bathroom. Glenn and I fed the starving little runt hard boiled eggs and this morning Adrien carried it outside. Whew. Well may we all be as lucky as that little raccoon and be surrounded by kindness. Have a good one. Peace.

June 17

Well dinner is cooking. One cocktail before I sit down and eat in a bit. Full facility tonight at Buddies which means both rooms are open, the big one as well as our usual rooms. Come dance at our pre-Pride pre-game thing. The queens are there it's just bigger and bigger. $10 at the door. Right now my life is about following the fucking trail of glitter till I find my way to heaven. Cheers!

June 19

Sitting on the balcony with Hélène sipping our before dinner cocktails. Splurged because it's Pride and bought a small bottle of Patron tequila. The balcony is calm and we can see lightning off in the distance. What a view from my chair out here right now. Be kind tomorrow, don't be a fucking asshole during pride, breathe and have a laugh at your own expense. Peace.

June 21

Resting on the balcony sipping a coffee. I skipped the weekly management meeting with the bosse's blessings so I could get an extra hour or two rest. Busy already, we are as ready at Buddies in Bad Times Theatre as we will ever be. Praying for nice weather as Pride is a lot about love under the blue skies and the canopy of invisible evening stars. Hope everyone is patient and kind to each other and over the next few days try and walk away from conflict. I hope I can do it too, because god knows right now it's everywhere. Live large within yourself love all you can and fuck those who can't. Peace.

June 22

The bunker has expanded its four footer occupants. We now have two long haired 10 week old sister and brother kittens. Pearl and Pirate. Pics start in a day or so. No Peace Now.

June 23

Woke up did my new chores associated with kittens, made coffee and sitting on the balcony listening to the weather. I love the rain and coolness of the day but am sad that it's happening this weekend of Pride. I celebrate Pride by being happy for those who love these few days of celebration. God only knows we need them we need to celebrate who we are right now when so many people like all of us are unable to even leave their homes without fear. I miss a lot of things that Pride was.

I acknowledge that things change just as I fucking have. What I am trying to say here? Enjoy these days and perhaps crowds and dance parties, like me. If not your thing still get up wish us all well and let the crazy fun happen. Well more coffee and to work.

I got a rude awakening that today was fucking Friday not Saturday. Smile at it all ignore the assholes and don't let the person in the mirror be an asshole either. Happy Pride and a heart tender Pride. Peace.

June 23

So just finished banging out on my acoustic guitar threw dinner in the oven, ready for Hélène at 10pm. Sipping a double ok truth, triple Jack and soda on the balcony and found out the kitten wrecking crew of Pearl and Pirate bail to safer ground under the couch, as soon as the first Conga drums start for Sympathy for the Devil from the Rolling Stones album Beggars Banquet. 40 years later still my go to album. Well all boring here, beautiful night enjoy it and breathe deep. Be kind. Peace.

June 24
So the beats coming out of the 519 park and Church St are smashing the air around us as we sit up here on our balcony. Wouldn't want it any other way. I was talking to a friend of mine yesterday he is a poet and songster and we were talking of life as it is for us as we are only a year difference in age. As we reflected on it all I said that part of our job here is to try and soften hearts. I like that as did he and that said let's try and soften some hearts today. Stay focused on kindness and Peace.

June 26

Well another Pride has come and gone. I worked my gay ass off all weekend serving a monsoon of thirsty queers and am now joyfully having a day of rest and reflection

a huge thanks and shout out to the Buddies crew for throwing the most epic parties/shows/performances and being the magical and inclusive space that I have been privileged to be a part of for 22 years and counting...what a great end to a fantastic season... WE DID IT... AND WE DID IT WELL! Cheers Queers!...I FORGOT HOW FUCKING CUTE TWO KITTENS CAN BE AS THEY DESTROY EVERYTHING IN THE BUNKER. LOVE THEM BOTH. PEARL AND PIRATE THE WRECKING CREW.

June 26

sitting on the balcony with Hélène and two of the older
        four footers.
The kittens wore themselves out and are sleeping
        under my
reading chair in the bunker living room.

I am in full sun so my girl brought out my hat and
        sunglasses with a glass of
Guinness for me.

She is a keeper.

I have ice packs on my feet and I am reading my own
            little chap book. I am
reading it in amazement that the stories and poems
            and daily updates were
given to me, something I intercepted and now
            interpreted. So thankful for
the gift of words and also the gifts of song riffs when
            they are sent my way.

Back at work tomorrow so going to ride the sun into
            the twilight. Breathe
deep in delight for your life and work towards your
            freedom. As always be
kind and Peace.

June 26
Thank you thank you to every one of you Pride
loving fuckers. xoxo
My feet hurt but what a
day to make them sore…

JULY

July 2
Morning feeding time two kittens two dogs two people all in the kitchen.

July 6

Thank you for all those amazing birthday wishes from amazing people. Also thank you to the two police officers who wished me happy birthday after I was too fucking drunk to figure out how to turn the bunker alarm off and sadly they had to come to my door and ID me and make sure I was ok. Fucking 63 going on 23. Cheers…

SLOUCHING TOWARDS WOMANHOOD
STORIES & POEMS

Introduction   Patricia Wilson 2019

Suddenly one day it hit me as I continued to write my essays, which reflected and explored my seemingly haphazard journey towards becoming physically female and the realization that once the process has been physically achieved the reality is more than the fantasy of what being female actually is. I will never be a 13 year old girl or a young woman negotiating the gauntlet of what women born women understand but for them seems impossible to share and to make others understand as though the women speaking and screaming have no voices at all. Still then, some women will never be what I was and what I am happily now a woman, but a woman with gaps of childhood experience so I must negotiate my sudden physical reality without a history of anything more than hearsay and a misread history to guide me.

My journey towards femaleness encompassed me both physically and psychically in the beginning, I always truly believed, and had somehow convinced myself that the journey there, that special life affirming trip was hard, but fairly easy and without much pain because I felt I was where I was and other than a few life lessons all was good and on track. Then after I started writing some essays around my life and where it was and where it went and where I ended it up I began to see that perhaps the damaged simplicity of it all may not be as steady and true as I had once thought.

Well, in actuality, not even close to fucking true at all. I have a standard reply when people ask me when I am going to "write the book about my life." What I believed until a short time ago to be a truth came to light in my reply, which was "it would be boring and no one would want to read the story once they started into it." I felt that I had no drama or things of interest around and inside of the stories of "the book" that would make it readable. Truth is told I still believe that, but what I don't believe now is that it was easy and painless for me. The reality and the truth of it all, which I knew, but had not defined, or perhaps admitted to myself until one day when again Hélène softly confronted me with "write that book" and I blurted out of my mouth "I can't write that book. I am afraid of the truth. I am afraid of my truth".

Now as I have written more of the essays, and they grow from the page at the very moment as I am writing, I realize the battered door is dented and crooked on my side from me trying to keep the truths behind the door, and the other side of the door, the side I can see or will let any one see is dented and crooked from the truths trying to see the light of day and feel the sunshine, the shining light if you will, of freedom. Overnight they, the truths that I had hidden away and denied or forgotten for so long suddenly became revived and had or have a life and destiny of their own outside of my perception of who I was and what my life had been. The door is not open, the door is only slightly ajar, but there is the big foot of a denied truth wedged between the frame and the door and it will never be closed again. The truth is peering out and its sloppy watery light starved eyes are hungry for the light and all that is the truth - those eyes want more.

The emotional distance and the physical distance combined with the face to face, toe to toe reality of the here and now, and my realization that the truth - my truth - has chased me.

It all confronts me on paper, and in the written and spoken word, the reality that I have been since I was a conscious child till moments ago, afraid of my truth.

The Stairs
previously published in 'geeks, misfits and outlaws; short fiction (editor Zoe Whittall), 2003, McGilligan Books, Toronto

Exhausted, I had just stepped off the bus, having been on tour for months. The band had actually pushed me awake and off the fucking bus, right in front of my door. Now I was slam stepping up the stairs towards my third floor apartment. I had half a bottle of beer in my pocket, a suitcase in one hand and a guitar in the other. As I hit the second floor to start my final assent, there it fucking was, a vagina, sitting on the stairs.

I stopped dead.

Not, I realized, because I was afraid. After all, I had a vagina, my girlfriend had one and I had spent a lot of my life at close quarters with many a vagina. What made me stop dead in my tracks was the turmoil in my thoughts. Like an adding machine, my brain began screaming out the numbers and types of intoxicating substances I had consumed over the last few months. One of those magic pills or powders had to be the reason for the twat sitting on the stairs in front of me. I am using the word twat as an added description for Miss Vagina; this was one tough looking vagina. I'll tell you. Picture a Miss Potato Head, with a vagina for the head, pierced and wearing motorcycle boots on these toothpick like legs, along with a leather vest, some weird custom made sunglasses (how else would they stay on, if they were not custom made)?

Then believe it or not, the damn thing pulled out a cigarette, offered me one, and lit the fucking thing. Now, I have seen a vagina blow smoke before, this is not a new thing for me. That vagina in the past, blowing smoke, was attached to a stripper who put the cigarette to those special V lips and right in front of my eyes took a drag and expelled the smoke. To finish the stripper story, she would then offer the cigarette to a customer who was instructed to put it in his or her mouth and stand perfectly still. You guessed it. She pulled out this huge bullwhip and sent that smoke flying across the room. This was the first time, however, I had ever seen a vagina in leather purposely light up. As the twat took a deep drag of the cigarette and blew a white cloud of smoke in my general direction, it began speaking to me in a sputtery, airy way.

"You live upstairs?" It asks.

I can't believe I'm fucking answering.

"Yes."
"It seems like a nice building," Miss Vagina or Miss Pussy or Miss whatever the fuck at this point, says to me. Now a thought rushes through my mind, I start to hyperventilate into a panic attack. Suppose this "nice building" kind of talk from Miss Vagina was a prelude to it moving into the building, into my building. I don't know why it freaked me, just a knee jerk reaction, I guess. I mean it's not as though I fit in as your normal everyday apartment dweller either, and there are

people who live here that look at my girlfriend and I with disdain or fear. So in spite of my common sense I'm ashamed to say that the pure fear of something, or someone freakier than me and outside my huge mental catalogue of freakiness, caused me to react badly. In response to Miss Vagina's statement, "Seems like a nice building," I replied, very sure of myself, "I don't know, the building's got its problems."

"Oh really?" comes the reply in a way that sends shivers down my spine. It had the sound of, the air of, " I know the owners and I'll be sure to tell them you said that." Fuck, fuck, fuck, what have I done? What was I doing talking to a sputtering vagina smoking on my stairway, and I say it again, my fucking stairway? Suddenly the stairway dweller bounces up onto its feet using those amazingly spindly legs and heads down the stairs towards the door. I can hear the clomp, clomp, of the boots as they hit each stair and I hear the door screech open and slam shut. At this point I am tempted to follow the leather-clad vagina and do some weird detective work, but my brain and body has had enough over the last few months and certainly the last few minutes.

I was so tired my eyes began watering. I was standing on the stairway, steps from home, staring down the stairwell. Starting back up toward the apartment I began rationalizing the encounter with the vagina. By the time I reached my door I was laughing at what the mind can do to you under different experiences and substances. I unlocked the door, stepped into the room with our happily barking dog running between my legs over and over again. I dropped everything on the floor and fished out the beer in my pocket and finished it as I was heading to the bedroom. My girlfriend, with a very sleepy voice says "Hi honey, welcome home." I said to her, "How are you? Man, I missed you really bad."

"Me too hon, love you" she whispers sleepily.

"Love you too, baby, see you in the morning," I say, as I fall into a deep, exhausted sleep.

I woke next morning to the wonderful smell of breakfast being made, a nearly daily ritual in our house for over ten years. I stumble from the bedroom to bathroom to kitchen and sit down at the table.

"Morning honey," we both say at the same time. I continue with "You would not believe how tired I was last night. I thought I saw a vagina dressed in leather sitting and smoking on the stairway."

"Oh, you met Valerie," she says.

I trip to my feet speechless, trying to say "Are you fucking crazy, a talking, smoking leather-wearing vagina and with the name Valerie?" The words won't leave my completely dried up mouth. Struggling to get my breath and speak, I look out the window. I see Valerie the Vagina on her scooter, with a smoke dangling from her mouth pulling up to our building.

In the proper light

The violence of the air does not touch you
The warmth of your breath is not my truth

In the proper light of day
Between the shadow and the ray
You can maybe see
the shimmering
Of ghosts dogging your trail
A reflection or glance
proclaim them
Between the shadow and the ray
You can perhaps hear
the wind of wings
Of angels soaring
with your breath
In the proper light of day
Between the shadow and the ray
In a sliver of darkness between
Concrete side by side
You can hear the
Swaying whispers
Of ancient dreams

I am only 61

I am 61
Some things are gone
For me

Never to be revisited
Never to be experienced
Yet I am a true survivor

True to myself because of the shining
of life/love of others
I am not at a crossroad

My path has been chosen
I am   I am not finished
I am not diminished

Digital

Digital time don't clock my minutes
Digital time isn't mine
Digital time moves the masses
Digital time keeps its own time
But not mine But not mine

I have no time for digital time

It leaves me cold and unsold
Digital time has its own agenda
Digital time shines its steady unholy light
Digital time shines on the sacred night
Digital time keeps its own time

But not mine But not mine

I have no time for digital time
It leaves me cold and unsold
Digital time is quiet and cunning
Digital time seduces
it is a lazy time

Trinidad Colorado

When I arrived in Trinidad, Colorado I had an appointment with Dr. Biber for an examination in his office before I was admitted to the hospital. He gave me a physical as expected, then told me to lift up the gown and show him the male anatomy. He reached over grabbed the fucking thing, pulling it tight, and said something along the lines of "oh good, lots of it there, it's going to make a good vagina." I was mortified but he wasn't wrong in his vagina prediction. Can't make this shit up.

Colorado Greyhound

So there I was, six days after my reassignment surgery and it was getting time to head back home to what I knew would be another emotional roller coaster. Thinking back there was very little support close to me for my decision to move forward with my life in the only way I saw possible. In the days around my journey to Trinidad, Colorado for the surgery, even those people who I thought were with me as I transitioned became frightened and withdrew, as it seemed suddenly so drastic to them. I heard from a number of people around me at the time, which simply amounted to verbal diarrhea - "we just thought it was a phase a little quirk you had." Anyway the surgery was done, I was happy, the doctors and nurses were happy and pleased for me, and Dr. Biber the surgeon said "It was one of the smoothest surgeries he had ever done, almost like it was meant to be right from your beginning." Good to hear whether it was a standard line or not it didn't matter to me at that time.

So the thing was I had exhausted my finances to get to Colorado. The extra cash I had to get back to the airport by car, then home was depleted on an unexpected medical cost. All I had was my plane ticket home and $40 dollars in cash. So I had to call a friend of mine to wire me enough money for the hours long bus ride to the little airport in Pueblo, Colorado where a very small commuter plane would take me to the Denver Airport. From Denver I would catch my flight to

Detroit and then be ferried home over the Ambassador Bridge to Windsor. Although my actual home, my abode was in deep jeopardy because I had moved forward and received my life saving surgery.

On the way six days earlier to undergo the surgery, I had taken a car from Pueblo to Trinidad and the hospital so that I would have as smooth a trip as possible. Now broke, except for enough borrowed money to take the bus to the airport, I was weak, bandaged, and obviously panic stricken about the whole situation. Although I could have stayed in Trinidad and lived for a while as I was asked by a technician that was part of the surgery process, who thought I was so beautiful and well spoken and Canadian too. He asked if I would like to move in with him for a few months or more. Fucking hell I just got my surgery and already a couple days in a handsome tranny chaser cowboy was offering me a chance to move onto his ranch with him. I must say, knowing what I was headed for when I got home, I did not say no right away. But alas I did turn it down as I pictured missing tranny girls chained up in a barn somewhere in rural Colorado. Yikes!

Remember I was on a lot of painkillers for the first couple of days and the mind can wander. Still perhaps if I had said yes I would be currently hosting a cooking show on some cable network in Trinidad, Colorado, about Midwest cooking and horse grooming.

It was a delicate time, as I almost had to stay another day or two because I had not learned to pee yet, and they would not release me till I had lowered the amount of urine in my bladder. It was a shock to me that for two full days I could not figure out how to pee. I was swollen of course and a little high from the pain killer drugs but peeing felt different. I had no idea what my new equipment was supposed to feel like when peeing. Different muscles were being used and just a whole different thing happening down there. Of course this created more panic in me because, as I said, I had cleaned out every cent I had. Even my family could not be called on to help me with money for the extra stay if it was necessary as I had not told them where I was, as they were so against this process.

So as the release date grew closer and closer and I was finally allowed out of bed to walk around slowly, and to try and relieve myself, which was complicated because I had to place an apparatus over the toilet that would collect my pee and then they could measure it. Still not a moment of regret passed through me and I smiled through this dilemma of the "no pee for me chapter." Did I mention that the hospital was also a teaching hospital for the area and many new doctors and nurses were being trained throughout my sojourn at the hospital. I saw so many new training doctors and nurses, all who are probably now retired and riding horses in the Colorado hills. I mention this only in passing as I remember now how they chose to remove the excess urine from my bladder. I was lying in bed after another unsuccessful trip to the washroom and three nurses came in to say hello and ask how I was doing. Let me say here that the staff at the hospital including the nuns who were on staff at that time were sweet, amazing and completely comforting and confirming. I recognized them as they entered the room as they had been taking care of me from the time I entered the hospital. The other nurse I did not recognize but because it was a teaching hospital I thought nothing of it. The nurse asked me how it was going as far as my "no pee chapter" was concerned and I said "Not so well." She nodded and said that sadly they were going to have to check to see how much liquid was in my bladder and remove some of it. Of course it did not dawn on me what was involved in this until they introduced me to the new nurse trainee and told me she was going to catheterize me to remove some of the liquid in my bladder. Quickly in a flash both nurses were at either side of me as I lay on the bed resting gently, but firmly holding my arms and legs down as the trainee nurse came toward my brand new pee hole with a catheter needle and apologizing as she moved in shakily for the deed. She got it down after the third fucking time and with almost little bloodshed but lots of *what the fuck!* on my part as, let's face it, my new pee hole was still swollen and tender from its fairly recent creation. So bottom line was the doctor came in and said "I think we can allow you to shower tomorrow. The hot water will relax your muscles and you will urinate." I did. They checked again and it went much smoother and I signed the release forms.

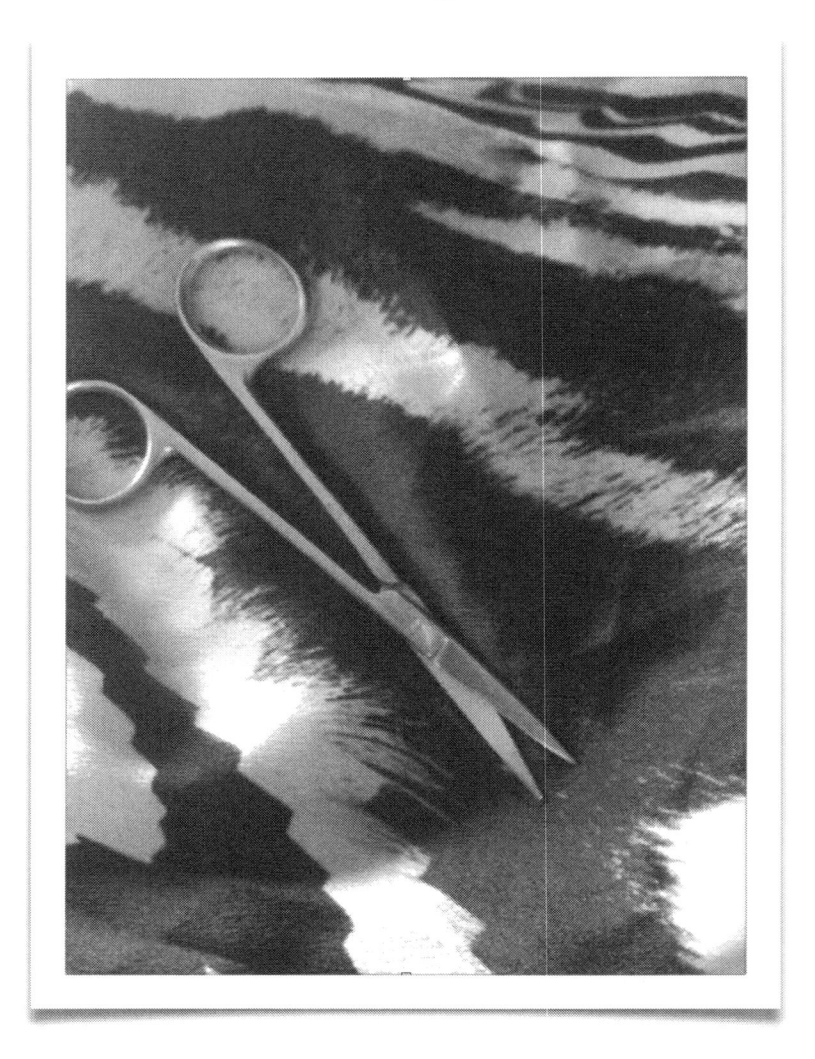

So as I packed and the nurses and the rancher bid me farewell and let me know that the doctor who had done the surgery was out on his day off, riding his horse in the mountain and said to say good bye and wished me good wishes and good luck. Sadly, years later, in his 80s, my surgeon was riding in the mountains and fell off his horse. From the story I heard from a truthful source, he hit his head and died a short time later. He died just shortly after my mother who also died in her 80s. This made me think both were part of the person who I am today. When I heard of his death I felt like an orphan of mind, body, and soul so to speak.

Upon release from the hospital I called a cab from the administration office where I paid the remainder of the *over $10,000 six day hotel stay* as I called it, and as a joke I had asked for the tweezers and the scissors that they had used on me since my bill showed I had paid for them. When the charges went through I was handed, with a friendly smile, both items in a little plastic bag.

I had booked another night in Trinidad, Colorado so I could gather myself together before hitting the road on a bus that I was terrified to take to the small airport in Pueblo Colorado and begin a journey that would take me back to Windsor where my private Stephen King-like circus would continue.

I arrived at the hotel and it was actually more of a motel with a dining room. So after packing early, so I could catch the bus early, I went to the dining room to eat some early dinner. The place was empty except for a few kids and an angry waitress who all let me know that they knew why I was in their town and that they were not happy about it. As I had now lost my appetite, I got up paid my bill and headed to the door and was even followed outside with shouts of freak, queer, and maybe even fag being thrown my way. I bet you're surprised the shout of tranny wasn't thrown in there too. Remember back then it was not in common usage, especially in that mostly red neck unsophisticated place in the world at that moment. They could not have had the tranny magic word that many of us later owned and loved. Which has now changed along with many other views around tranny and gender.

I went back to my room and tried to sleep between my dilations as they were necessary every so often, but even my nerves were pumping the adrenaline through my wide-awake brain. I picked up the bus outside of the motel and with my Sony Walkman and a small overnight bag I walked up the steel stairs of the bus towards a sneering driver. I paid my fare and turned towards the inward sanctuary of the bus to find a seat for the hour or more ride. As I headed down the aisle I could see that the bus was over three quarters full of locals. As I walked down the aisle after almost falling on my face, as the bus driver had seemed to purposely speed up to try and make me fall, which elicited a busload of laughter, I looked for a seat to just relax and count my time to when I would be away from this fucking place. Every time I chose an empty seat the person beside it would put their hand on it or a lunch pail or a shopping bag and shake their head. You get the picture I am sure. So almost in tears I went to the front of the bus expecting help from the driver but he said nothing. So I thought, ok, I will just stand here at the front of the bus till we get to the airport. He looked at me with his continued sneer and said: "You're blocking my view, sit down there." He pointed to the metal stairs beside his chair and every time he stopped for a passenger pick up or drop off I had to get up, grab my bag and go down the stairs, never letting go of the door handrail, as I was afraid if I left the bus for a second he would slam the bus doors in my face and take off down the highway, with his sneering laughing passengers, and I would be stuck in bum fuck Colorado with no money and nowhere to go.

After awhile, and I no longer can remember or care to remember how long we were on the road, the bus pulled into a small little town to pick up more passengers and for a restroom and snack break. I had a perfect view as we came into town as the steel stairs that I was sitting on had two doors with long windows on each door that swung open. The town seemed clean and almost inviting, semi-busy with people walking on the street, window shopping, and as the bus stopped at a stop light I saw a lovely young couple sitting in the window of a little restaurant holding hands and staring into each others eyes. An intimate warm moment, and I still remember it to this day.

Not so long ago I was headed to Guelph University with my dear friend and collaborator to read poetry and prose to a class there, and we were on a bus from Toronto to Guelph. As we passed through one of the small towns on the way I suddenly realized that this small Ontario town looked just like the small Colorado town the bus pulled into that day so many years ago. The difference was the perspective of course, as here in this year I was seated on a comfortable seat next to someone I loved and they loved me - compared to sitting on a set of steel bus stairs with people sneering and almost spitting on me. I have no idea why they did not spit on me as I did expect it at any moment as they exited at their stops and it felt as though the comfortable seated riders of the bus would break into applause if they had spat on me.

On that long ago Colorado bus ride, as the automatic transmission downshifted, slowing down to the rest stop and vibrating, the bus and its steel stairs, that had for maybe over an hour become my seat, and believe me I felt every vibration through every incision, and right then and there I knew I was in trouble.

I had to pee. Long before washroom debates in the here and now of this story I had a situation around having to pee.

Let me say here, in almost 30 years since my surgery it's been rare, other than an occasional questioning small town paranoid woman, that I have had washroom problems. But right then on that bus ride every person knew my story and it mattered to them very much. As I stepped out of the way of the passengers as they exited the bus to get snacks and to go pee, more than one woman said to me, "Which bathroom are you using?" Bone fucking chilling to me as I felt as though the ride had dislodged my bandages and it felt like I was bleeding again from my surgery and my bladder was feeling full. I knew that if I went to the bathroom I would be a few minutes to readjust the bandages afterwards, so I devised a plan to go after I was sure my fellow bus passengers had done their bathroom duties. Ah, sounds so simple, but the bus driver, as he passed me to go for a coffee and his bathroom break, looked me in the eyes, and if his looks could kill, said - "If you're not here when I come back I am leaving you behind." I stayed put - in pain, bleeding, thirsty as fuck, but I was not going to be stuck in this fucking place with people like this. I would rather have died on those fucking stairs, and make those people have to get out of the bus and dig a shallow grave for my new female self in the Colorado countryside so I could fly with the tranny angels in heaven. Fuck them. Ok, so I stayed on the bus now feeling faint and still I had to pee. As the bus pulled out to hit the highway again the bus driver said - "oh by the way do not use your Walkman as it's bothering me and some of the passengers, it's too loud, turn it off." Of course the only thing I had to distract me was now suddenly a liability on this ride from fucking hell.

So I made it to the airport and I had purchased a round ticket when I had first arrived, and this was before intense airport security, so I had very little trouble once I walked away from Satan's bus. The thing is I was bleeding, and not in a good way, and I wasn't even in Denver yet, which was just over two and half hours to Detroit. I was afraid to pee, as I feared that once I removed the bandages I would start bleeding heavier and who knows. So I set my mind to pee when I got home, that was it. So they called for departure and as I headed to the plane I looked up and it was just small enough that I had to climb a fucking ladder to get into the demon prop plane.

I made it to Denver and there are other stories to tell of the arrival but I got on a supposedly over sold flight to Detroit. I was drenched in sweat and white from loss of blood and exertion. I got into my seat and closed my eyes feeling sick to my stomach, wondering if ,after all I had been through to get to this point, I was going to die somewhere in the air over the fucking United States. I remember in my dazed frame of mind I said out loud "no regrets." I don't know if the steward passing me on his way to "first class" heard me or not, but he tapped me on my shoulder and said, "Sweetie I know your story come with me." He grabbed my bag from the overhead and helped me to first class and opened me a bottle of red wine and made me food and sat with me till we got to Detroit. As I was leaving the plane he said, "you're so brave, good luck" - and he asked one of the stewardesses to get me to where I needed to be. Over 30 years ago there were gay angels flying our skies.

GUELPH
the train

It's 6am in the morning. David Bateman and I - I like to call him Dr. David Bateman - have a reading in Guelph at 11:30 am. I have not slept 30 seconds because travel and deadlines are enough to keep me awake for my whole life. But at six am I got up and said fuck it, I'm going to start my day without the sleep and see what happens. Because as Patti Smith says, paraphrasing her words - "sometimes lack of sleep leads to subtle awarenesses."

So my insomnia created a situation where I forgot the exact time when Mr. Bateman asked me to be at his place in the cab. So the first time in years I am early and sitting outside his apartment an hour earlier than I should have been, in a cab calling him when he could have still been sleeping or having a shower. The cab driver's saying to me "I don't understand why I am here when nobody's coming out the door." I'm trying to convince the cabbie to drive up and down the street from one end to the other, and finally David came out the door, got in the cab, and very politely looked at me and said "No worries we are forty-five minutes ahead of where we're supposed to be."

I am carrying a walking stick and can barely walk and we make it through Union Station only to sit down in front of the little convenience store just outside the ticket booth and David went into get water. And it started, you would have thought this old tranny sitting there on a bench with her cane and her little suitcase was the only attraction in the city of Toronto that morning. People circled around to get a second glance.

Of course I have always been paranoid so while David is in the store I thought perhaps it's me. Then David came out and sat down and said "what are these fucking people looking at?" And then in a louder voice - he said "Who do they think they are? Who do they think we are when they have such little lives to begin with."

And as the two people on either side of us got up and moved to another seating station. David and I sipped our water and made fun vicious conversation about the people who were totally enjoying the Bateman/Wilson show in Union Station.

So the time comes when we must move and of course I am using my stick to get around and have to limp all the way to the train tracks which are up three and a half flights of stairs. The people around us all had their nine to five hours to be at and were pushing and shoving and stabbing at each other to get to the train to get to their preferred seating. We actually had to step over a body that was slowly bleeding out into the stairs below after being al little bit too slow to get to the train.

So David and I finally made it to the train and sit down and immediately fantasized that we are on a magical mystery tour that was going to change our lives…but it was Guelph!

As the industrial wasteland zipped by the windows and the odd used parking lot and another train going the opposite direction past our window and you saw the bloated unhappy faces staring at you as they came from the opposite direction. David and I looked at each other soulfully, looked into each others eyes and said, 'We could cancel.'

the GO Bus

After the many fantasies that a train brings, the reality of the 90 minute bus ride to Guelph sinks in. David and I were both shattered. I was sleepless, David had not had enough art in the last twelve hours to make him stable. So the problem being is I am using a stick and we have to run down 70 stairs or use a slow elevator to get to the GO Bus that will take us to the university. We took the elevator to the bus lanes but the bus was still a long walk for us. Of course it was probably under a hundred yards, but when you're using a stick and have no sleep it seems like 20 miles. David wrapped a kerchief around his head and put the bags in the crook of his arms, and all I remember is the hot click of his heels and the flash of the bus as he ran along the platform to prevent the bus from leaving us behind.

Ten minutes later I get to the bus to hear David negotiating with the driver because the Presto pass did not register the correct amount as we missed the terminal for the complete payment for the journey. The driver whose family had come to say hello and stood outside the bus watching him negotiate with David scowled at me as I stumbled along. The driver took one look at me and seemed to be saying with his look that he was never going to win this battle with a fag and a tranny and a walking stick..

As we were driving it soon became a scenic route to the university. As I sat there in my insomniac stupor wondering if I would make it through the day, suddenly the view blurred in my mind between Colorado and Guelph. As we pulled into a small Ontario town the ride suddenly became a small town outside of Pueblo, Colorado on my way home from my sex change surgery 30 years ago.

As my dysphoric blurry vision occurred and we pulled out of the little town, I looked at David and began speaking to him in 'tranny' tongues about the journey home from Trinidad, Colorado where my surgery had taken place. In my stream of consciousness stories of I continued relating to David about how the emotion was triggered by the scenery, and to think that David and I were not being our bus fare to be there, just a flat fee. It was a journey for art and memory.

the University of Guelph food court and campus

We arrive at Guelph and we are met by one of Sky's students on the property. As we enter into the student commons I suddenly think of the last time I was in a student common. I was on a radio tour for my band Crackpuppy with a publicist who was older than me and so creepy that the whole time he talked under his breath about the young students we were passing to get to our show. One of the creepiest men I have ever met.

But David and I needed food, especially since I hadn't eaten since the night before. We found something that looked something like food. I ordered white pasta with no flavour specifically. I could not finish it so I gave it to David. In a daze in a chair surrounded by twenty-year-olds. As we left the cafeteria our host explained everything we were looking at, from the cannon in the outdoor common area to each old building we passed. I remember looking at seven million children walking towards me thinking that I lost my way and the tranny in wonderland was lost in an anthill…

the reading

The hallowed halls of an older building which suited the older readers was to take place on the third floor. Like Marianne Faithful Patricia is using a stick and cannot make it up the stairs. Dr. Gilbert being caring and fully aware as he usually is, as I told him in emails about my stick, went upstairs to one of Canada's leading playwrights Judith Thompson and asked if she could switch classes on the main floor so that the limping tranny with a cane did not have to go up three flights of stairs. Ms. Thompson and I had met before through Buddies In Bad Times Theatre. She looked at me and said "I completely understand. I hope you feel better." She melted my heart with her kindness.
The first sign I noticed was that there were three headbangers among the students sitting in the big open room. I was wearing the colours of a metal band. David and I read very well, people responded

appropriately, and understood what we were saying and seemed to enjoy what we were offering.

The reading ended and many many questions helped David and I enlighten our work to ourselves - and hopefully the students. Finally at the very end two headbangers came up to me and said "You were in a metal band, what band?" and continued to question me on my rock and roll paraphernalia that is my daily wear - goes to show you poetry can't survive without rock n roll.

on the road

So we were getting a ride home from one of Sky's TAs, back to Toronto, so we didn't to have to incur more costs for the reading. We stopped at a diner for lunch. David had well-deserved beer. I had a milkshake.

the ride home

There had been some controversy about a piece Dr. Gilbert published in a blog that centred around the theatre I work for and the people I know. Since I love both the theatre and the man who hired me to work at that theatre, Dr. Gilbert, it was a complicated situation. and on the ride back from Guelph he was talking to the Globe and Mail about the incident while David and I were in the back seat. I being very aware of our situation did the most intelligent thing I could do. I put my fingers in my ears. I could hear none of the conversation.

We arrived at my apartment building at the back entrance. They let us out. They hugged me and they thanked me, gave us all their accolades and I can sincerely say that I felt with everything that had happened I felt fulfilled and successful. Not successful in the way that I was going to own a boardwalk in Atlantic City but successful in the way that some dying person thirty years from now with their last breath will say, "I remember a reading in Guelph where my life was changed."

this is it

My first day transitioning at work. I am up at 6am. I had practiced and gone to restaurants dressed as a woman in preparation for this and I have been on hormones for four weeks, and contrary to what anybody will tell you, the hormones have done fuck all in four weeks. I have not turned into the Marilyn Monroe character I thought I would be with the onset of hormones. I stare into my little make-up mirror sitting on the table that has different shades for morning evening and afternoon. It is six o'clock in the morning and I am about to start my first day as a woman in a job where I have been male for four years. My job was as a welder and I was about to enter into a small town factory after leaving on the Friday a male and coming back two days later as female. I was terrified. But determined.

I had notified my superiors and my closest friend at the factory and I ventured in after loading my credit card for women's clothes over the weekend. I got out of my Volkswagen 1978 beetle and thank god I had jeans boots drag queen makeup a wig and a will to change my life. Needless to say by the end of the day I was in two fist fights, one yelling match and a smile for the future.

groceries

By this time, early in my transition, it was clear that no one was going to help me, and it dawned on me that I needed booze, cigarettes, and groceries. Agoraphobia was setting in as it's not easy for a small town 'drag queen' wandering the streets. I am often seen as a drag queen not as a woman. I ventured into the grocery store. Before I left my apartment I had convinced myself, staring into the mirror, that no one would notice me as I shopped for eggs, meat, and cleaning supplies. I was wrong.

the bar

After six months I felt I could venture out into the nightlife. Not the disco nitelife but a local gay friendly bar where I could sit and eat at the bar and enjoy a cocktail and talk to the bartender who I knew very well, who knew my story and was more than happy to have me. In this bar, unbeknownst to me, I met my future spouse playing pool together. But we did not hook up until four years later. I was sitting at the bar wearing what I thought was the coolest outfit - black jeans, a three quarter length red leather coat, two inch heel boots, my makeup impeccable. Sitting at the bar were two men to the side of me. I heard them say "Do you think thats one of those transexual people?" This is more than 30 years ago. Thinking back, I did not think cavemen knew the word transsexual, and the one caveman said to the other, "The only way we can tell is by the size of their hands." I saw them look at my hands and they looked at each other and said "Nope not a transexual. Just a lesbian."

Mom

My mother had a problem with my transition from the very beginning. I spent ten to 12 years barely talking to my mother. And my sister, we spoke, but not super close, and she had children and a husband who did not understand due to children etc. But one day my sister was staying down with my mother when my mother was in her mid 70s. After 25 years of struggling with my transition, and who I am, and my sister says to my mother - "Don't you think it's the bravest thing anyone could ever do on their own?" And my mother stopped and thought, that suddenly because I had traveled halfway across North America to have my surgery, no help, nobody went with me - nobody helped me - afraid of flying, my mother was counting on my fear of flying that it would never happen. My sister said to my mother "Are you willing to lose one of your children just because you don't understand them." It was an epiphany for my mother and things turned around immediately.

My mother called me and said, "I want you to know I think you are the bravest person I have ever known. I don't understand what you have done but I love you and I know you're very intelligent and you have thought this out." And from that day on my mother and I talked once or twice a day even though we were 250 miles away. I was in Toronto and she was in Windsor, and then in London, Ontario later in her life. And although I would visit there periodically I always had an expiry date on my arm and the time would come when she couldn't stand me anymore and she would throw me out of the city. But I'd be back.

hippies against trans

In 1976 I drove across the U.S. in a Cadillac. There were four of us and there was three days of travel. I had just started taking estrogen again. We got to California - Topanga Canyon - everybody seemed so loose and happy and open minded to everything. We visited my friends of many years who I had lived with in Windsor and had moved to Topanga Canyon. Over a couple of joints and a couple bottles of wine I told them about me and my duel with me and my male self and my female self and my estrogen. One of the women in the crowd I had known many years jumped out of her hippy chair made out of a door and said "What are you talking about, there is no female vibe from you, you just want attention!" As I looked over to their fireplace from the table, piled right up the chimney with crumpled up bags and garbage, I thought to myself - "There is far more garbage talking to me in the living room than in the fireplace."

They refused to support me and at one point during my stay they found a young blonde beautiful actress who they tried to hook me up with, thinking that she would fuck the transsexual out of me. But over a twenty-four hour marathon of Beatle movies we just decided to be girlfriends and I left California, to return many times after, but knowing what my true calling was.

You found Kahlo

You found her first
The strength the determination
It shone in front of you
Frida Kahlo called to you

A young girl filled with
Questions of self
Questions of where from here
Kahlo was yours long before
I explored her art

I knew of her
Diego surprised me
In Detroit a mural
But Frida was not
Part of a surprise

You found her she had to be
To a young girl struggling
In her art and place
Frida Kahlo

Frida Kahlo
All woman and artist
And far more
For you

For you
For many

Like you.

You were a young girl
In need of her
I never was
I would never be

I found Frida as my
Skin dried and wrinkled
With age

Not a young girl me
But something else
Now female
In need of Frida Kahlo
Like the young girl   I never was.

'Real'

Maybe in my early teens, I had already had estrogen, I had gone to the Clarke Institute. My girlfriend that I had been with since 17 helped me cross-dress for a photo for the Clarke. They wanted to see what I looked like as a female. You had to send a pic of you dressed in women's clothes which I did not do on a regular basis. So we were together a few years before she smartened up and found a wonderful man. A wonderful 'real' man and went with him and broke my heart. Just because you're a tranny doesn't mean you don't have a heart that cannot be broken.

We remained friends over the years and she was going into her masters for counselling at University of Windsor. This was the late '70s early '80s, before people knew what transexuals were. And her and I decided that if she was going to get her masters the least I could do was give her the story of my life for her research. We sat down and talked and talked and she submitted my whole life as her degree and got high marks. Not a lot of people had ever dealt with transsexuality at that time and she was supposedly counselling a real transexual, me. I gave her my story and she left me for a 'real' man.

First time onstage with a guitar in Toronto

It was at the Horseshoe Tavern and I had no idea what people would think of my band Crackpuppy. I was thinking the worst and hoping for the best. We were astounded, and we were told that later there was a review in the newspaper saying that they thought we were using another band and not Crackpuppy. But they were amazed by the band and how blistering the lesbian guitarist was. After reading that review I decided that even though I was asked to many times, I would never go for the trans thing for my band. It was always about the music. The most deviant thing about our band was that there were two queers and one lesbian up there onstage. That was it.

Buddies Bartender

The room is full of people who stop and stare and look at me and I look at them and we acknowledge all the forces allowing us to be in this environment considering what environments we might be in. Working at Buddies as a bartender takes the rough edges off me, teaches me more than I deserve to know.

my way and love
Had my had my way
But not todayayay

Learned of life
Through the eyes of love

Farsighted nearsighted myopic

How then could I
How then could I

How then could I live
A life straight and narrow

I saw passion and desire

As a life well loved
As a love well lived

Vietnam

The first time I saw a man and woman have sex was when I was on hash. They were deserters from the Vietnam War. I was in grade eight. An older woman who had a beautiful home and lived on her own, she was a grandmother. One day her grandson showed up from Ann Arbor Michigan. He had walked across the border in his full marine uniform and never went back to the United States. He had been in medical school and left and was immediately drafted. After going through boot camp he found out he was being sent to Vietnam, so he deserted and moved into his grandmother's house in Windsor. Suddenly the Vietnam war became part of my reality.

The thing with him moving into his grandma's house was that I was in grade eight, it was barely the 70's, and somehow I immediately endeared myself to them and their American family, and I received the nickname Ace. Every weekend they would come from Ann Arbor to visit their deserter brother. We would sit on his grandmas front porch and smoke grass and then hash and then LSD. I had a part time job delivering newspapers and my boss at the time came to talk to me about the papers not being delivered. But all I could do was stand on my front lawn and move in a circle in one spot because I was so high. He walked away frustrated.

The man that had deserted and moved to Windsor and found himself with the most beautiful girl I had ever seen in my life. He could not be with her in his grandmother's house so he rented a room on the main street of Windsor. I would go over three or four times a week and smoke hash and watch him chase flies around with an aerosol can and a lighter. One night as I was sitting at the table smoking hash he and his girlfriend had vigorous sex, almost touching my elbow as I sat there. The room was so small. I was barely out of grade eight at this point, and when they finished she stood up and I saw her naked, and her pubic hair was wet and was glistening and I thought that's what I should be.

Is it true?

Is it true is it true?
As John Giorno says
"You got to burn to shine"

Is it true? Is it true?
You have to lose to get
Lose a game to win a game

Is it true is it true?
You have to lose some cents
To gain a small little stash.

Lose on love to gain a friend

Is it true? Is it true
You have to lose a war
To gain a shaky truce
Is it true? Is it true
You must first lose to fear
To find that dusty true love

sunrises and street lights

I still haven't shaken off or changed or reshaped all my youthful hopes and dreams. Oh many have fallen away, some are barely recognizable in the bright light of daylight. And there is perhaps a blurring of purpose, caused by admittedly having seen a few sunrises in my time and quite a few glowing night street lights as well. Growing.

"mothers little helper"

I watched my mother go through (surrounded by doctors and caregivers) terrible pain from cancer of the lungs and the throat, and was dismayed at the taking away of her life-long prescribed drug which put her into a drug withdrawal dementia. Her pain was actually on a lower two level of one to ten, according to her, unless they tried to force feed her with a tube down her throat mostly closed by the tumour. We could hear her screams from down the hall until we got up and demanded they stop or find another way. My mother, a woman who worked as a stay at home mother in the 50s and 60s had been on valium, sometimes only a half of valium a day (mothers little helper) because of her nerves - whatever that was at any particular moment so there was an addiction to the drug that helped her function for over thirty or more years. Let's say I cannot remember valium not being part of her daily routine, not unlike Lemmy and his speed. The doctors and the nurses in their wisdom immediately cut her valium off as soon as she entered the hospital and she was terminal, so begins the withdrawal from her life long psyche walking stick. Horrible, cancer and its tentacles of despair and pain mixed with the absence of the valium. When I realized what was happening I demanded that they return her chemical walking stick immediately as did my sister who was and continues to be a force as strong and as pure and as hard of a shit kicker as our mother ever was. To paraphrase their response we were told, "No it's a drug and an addiction and must be dealt with." Being the reserved person I am I yelled "what the fuck she is fucking dying she is in pain and now you put her into withdrawal." At one point, the interns and nurses were speaking outside of her room in a group and said something to the effect "well what do you expect she smoked into her fifties that's the way it is." I heard this, my sister heard this, and so did her doctor who was a kind considerate man, who due to his outrageous schedule could only share his time in small amounts. When he heard this he literally exploded and began yelling generally at those guilty of the idle talk outside my mothers room. Reminding them they were "trying" to be doctors and that if they wanted to stay on his team they had better re-evaluate their attitudes towards the patients they were caring for. He went on to imply all patients deserve all their energy and to judge someone for their past was not their job and as a matter of fact he did not think that smoking was the major cause of her cancer since it had been almost forty years since she had smoked. So the cards were stacked against her, she was worn down from all the issues around her that I have laid out already, and then they were taking her into surgery if she was strong enough. Her strength was in her heart of hearts and her faith. As reflected in this moment from her hospital bed. The doctor came in and said Mrs Mitchell, (mom's new married name) "we can't say that you will survive the surgery if we do go ahead with it." Mom replied, "Doctor you should know I am not afraid, I have faith in my God and have absolutely no fear of dying or any fear of what the future could bring. I will live as long as God decides, not whether something happens on the operating table." I will tell you, I believe to this day she had no fear of death. She held fast that her belief in life after death and her faith would hold true even in her passing from this realm to the next. Her only fear was of what new torture the doctors had planned for her. Mom died without surgery in my sister's arms after my sister had lovingly said to her, "You can go mom, we will be alright, we love you." Mom I am told took a couple deep breaths and started to drift away, the nurses and doctors came to ask my sister, who was alone with her, if she wanted them to assist mom or let things take it course. Mom chose her own way to leave and the room in palliative care that was reserved for her never got used.

What does it take to look death in the eye like that - bravery, faith, whether a dying patient in a hostile hospital or care centre or a soldier on the hostile battle field.

Looking death straight on, fearing the pain but stepping forward into what at that moment is your lot in life. Not knowing the next step, leaving behind all you loved and have spent a life nurturing and caring for. To be simply human is the bravest act of all.

the gap
The gap between
Alive and Living
The gap between
Breathing and a Breath
The gap between
Seeing and SEEING

The gap between
Alive and Living
The gap between
Breathing and a Breath
The gap between
Seeing and SEEING

memories

When my father died I remember standing over his body still warm in the hospital bed and lovingly touching his still warm hand and saying out loud, at least you won't see the destruction of the world by war. That was what, 1977 or 1978, ask my sister for the exact date. I remember the emotion not the facts. That is my downfall as a writer. Because of this flaw all memories become fiction. We live in the past and create our lives according to the fiction that our memories fictionalize for us.

LSD acid trips & strong women
Do we question our big decisions. For me that could be fatal.

As I ate breakfast across the table from Hélène I paused between bites to glance over to my wrist to see whose hand was holding my favourite fork and suddenly in the pit of my stomach I felt what my eyes were seeing. As I looked at my wrist I saw my mothers wrist right down to the little bruises created from working through a shift. I thought wow this is almost like an acid trip - and what about LSD, somewhat a wonder that drug was for me back in the day. It allowed me to explore the questions of my gender without speaking to anyone or moving within what was a limited world for me back then. Limited because I could only be what people perceived me to be not what was boiling within me just below the surface.

That magical drug the soul opening LSD helped me to move inward beyond my sometimes-crippled sexuality. The older I became the less I understood my self my sexuality my slithering slouching humanness and with that little understanding came the realization I did not know at one point whether my gender dysphoria was from between the legs or from between the ears deep in my brain. LSD burned to the core and helped me understand that it was all that but more far more it was something I was born to explore not to just experience not just something to achieve something I would for ever and ever struggle to understand and journey to put it in a place within me around me and after me.

Truth is the acid was of course such a different part of my journey, my jumpstart to achieving a semblance of who I knew I was. Yet living in your head which is spiritually and psychically very cool and changes you forever in a good way, but still, it is not the actual crowbar that will help tear down the realities of day to day living so you can make physical changes. It is the understanding of your motives and truths that help put the crowbar into your hands that change your life. Back then it was all I could hope for a semblance of what I knew I was. The dream or wish to be human a fully realized human being both in mind and body was seemingly out of reach. So as so many of us do I settled on achieving the "I will settle for" attitude and moved that building block forward like a forgotten chipped chess piece that shows up in the junk drawer years after you have stopped playing chess. I mean I couldn't count how many times I had thrown this dream to become female into the junk drawer as like chess I felt I could never achieve the win because I could never understand the game. So why then, what at that moment made me make the move towards the "I will settle for what I can get" attitude? Well, it is a fucked up story but it had a bit of breathing divine motion in it and the angels of truth and sisterhood touched me.

Speaking of sisterhood my mom and my sister both

dear women and my mother's mom, my grandmother a presence in our immediate family for as long as I can remember. Although my sister was 10 years younger than me she was a force unto herself. There was little she would suffer it was not what she wanted and the battles to get her to grade school daily are legendary. My mother was so complex and was a very beautiful woman who was urged to go to Detroit and start a modelling career at 19 years old, which was out of her reach for many reasons. We had heard stories of youthful nervous breakdowns and outbreaks of screaming plate throwing - a truly emotional childhood misunderstood by her mother and siblings and punished for these outbursts rather harshly as the story was passed forward to me. My mother rarely spoke of her childhood except to say she grew up with bad nerves and loved her family especially her father (as a girl does) who died in his fifties from the result of a gas attack during the First World War He never fully recovered and he was surrounded by men who had been through the same ordeal.

The other thing which I will touch upon is the "rum running" my grandfather and grandmother partook of as they lived in a Canadian border city across from the very supposedly liquor free American city of Detroit. They had lived for a period in Detroit before moving to the Commonwealth, which is Canada. (They were British and Irish born citizens). The stories have been told before on how people ran booze to Detroit and its part of our history, and it's amazing. I just want to touch upon my mother telling me the stories of getting up in the morning and seeing money piled high on the kitchen table and watching her father divide the money into even piles and go out and distribute the money to vets and some under earning families. I always felt it was true as unlike the Kennedy's of Camelot in the United States there were no mansions or power as a result of having made booze running money.

My grandmother as long as I can remember worked cleaning a hotel to supplement her pension. We would meet grandma after her work which was around 1pm on Saturdays (my father worked Saturdays) and we would go to a little dark bar with huge round leather bank seats and mom and her mom would kibitz over a beer or two and the kids (my sister not yet born) would drink Shirley Temples which I remember mostly because of their stunning colour. It was the deepest colour of red and I was amazed that it could be in a glass to drink. Moving, as all of us kids grew older into grade school, mom who was well read very intelligent and always talked of being a writer, and I will tell you her letters were coveted amongst those she corresponded with. They were amazing and I still, as does my sister, have some stowed away somewhere. She was a beautiful woman writing beautiful things to those she loved. Ah, but the spectre of what we called back then, mom's bad nerves, never of course went away and as she was left alone while my father worked at the auto plant seven days a week. Self medication moved in and there were some tumultuous years for all of us, sometimes downright dangerous. Still an amazing woman who came into herself after my father died and went back to school, learned how to drive and was the Florence Nightingale to all her siblings who passed long before she did. A wonderful woman who even after self medication could suddenly be bedridden for seemingly no reason and it seemed more physical than anything else. Mom lived into her 80s and my sister and I talk of her with warm hearts and delightful memories.

My sister and I are very close and talk, well, now text almost everyday, we live two hours by train away from each other and she is an amazing woman herself. A Mother of two grown children that she nurtured and fought for on many battlefields. She is an amazing painter and her canvases are stunning. She gave it up to parent and is a partner in an all-encompassing marriage. She is still happily married and now is the mother of two kittens and a tiny little Weston pup. Here is the thing, my grandmother and mother and sister all were similar strong women and a while back my sister, after having bouts of physical letdowns, was diagnosed with MS a disease that affects you body and soul as it's a frustrating disease that can prevent you from doing what you want to. It's in the genes and runs usually through the women in a family. Strong women around me, role models, and I remember feeling secretly part of their sisterhood even though I never ever spoke of such things till it hit this page. A memory just filtered in from my childhood of walking down the street holding my mothers hand and my father carrying my brother and coming across a young mother herself on the sidewalk and her stopping us and saying to my mother as she looked at me and said "Oh a beautiful little girl why don't you let her hair grow, it's so short, and she has such beautiful hair." My dad grumbled almost yelled "That is my son and it's a boy." Next day, my hair, with me crying in the barbers chair, got a lot shorter. Weird how memories move themselves through you.

And I think of all the bars and bartenders and sisterhood. I was standing at a punk bar that was also a gay bar, which overtook the punk as more popular, but there were way more gay men there that night than punk rock lovers.

As I was standing by the pinball machine with my sunglasses, which in those days I wore day and night, and just home from my cross country drive and stay in America, by way of a Jack Kerouac Route 66 adventure where I was determined to hit California and a Big Sur Zen monastery when I got to the end of the road where a friend had moved, and perhaps I would meditate or whatever, rid myself of my desire to become female. I had made it almost there and I had a mystical cue or nudge on the train and turned around and never kept my appointment with the admissions monk. I had quit once again. This time for around eight months for the second or third time I had quit my estrogen and I knew there were still maybe signs of it on me so I was sensitive about the way I may have presented myself or was being perceived.

The pinball game was binging and chirping and I was losing being completely distracted by the band that had finished ten minutes before. A Detroit band with Ron Ashton on guitar from Iggy and the Stooges and a member of the Mc5 in the band as well. I loved Destroy All Monsters, such a great band. So as I stood there the same vision or memory that had turned me back from the monastery came upon me again rather suddenly and I felt weak in the knees and was thankful for the pinball machine to hang on to steadying myself against it.

So the boy child a baby barely able to walk and shift in the world is lying in the world he awakes to scratching at his bedroom window. Terrified he can't help himself he just can't fucking help himself he reaches out and throws the blankets to the floor and runs to the window and they are there waiting there for him and their eyes meet and the window glass melts, a hard haggard hand grabs him by the throat and magically puts the boy in this beings back pocket and as it climbs up the side of the house the little boy hears in its mind I am the good witch of women. Now you are ours and will be ours this is your beginning and your end the end of your maleness in this moment it is not a dream as you will discover. And the boy woke up changed and full of things that were not there when he went to bed. And a new life began that morning.

my view of skin

My view of skin
Not the baby soft perfect
Not the sweet sex sweaty
Not the child bruised

Or the knife, glass or bullet
Damaged
Skin of the nightly news

I look and touch my skin
My own medal of time

We have fought the hard battle
Of birth
Of youth
Of ourselves

We have not
We have not
Survived without the Scars

sad quote

You are just a sad quote on the human race
Our art must be our freedom
I admonish you for your bleary eyed
Hate

admonish admonish I point my finger
At you and the destruction by you
Of freedom, nature and of the lost and discarded.
I weep for life I weep for all it is

3X
Three times in the dream I dream within
the dream an escape by car in the dark driving a 40's
chief fire car blinded by the bush around me

I spun out and out of the darkness three nuns arise and
walk towards me.

I wake up.

bloodied hands silent scream

The violence of the air does not touch you
The warmth of your breath is not my truth
The deserts of life keep spreading
Swirling and moving swirling movie
A dance of righteousness
The difference between you
And me the difference between
Right and wrong is sometimes
Simply a matter of opinion.

I look down my hands are bloodied
I look down your hands are blooded
We look up into each other's eyes
We scream the silent scream
No one is innocent when you look
Away away far away from

Pregnant

The air touching me is dangerously
Pregnant with conscious thought
Spinning to breath rhythms
Like a dog whistle
Unheard but felt by the dogged

Essay of life; three chords
If I could live within three chords
A three chord chant or dance
Three chords left lying on paper.

As I have moved into my 61st year I am noticing and feeling the silence of the air more and more.

A deep breath is more than a deep breath I am more aware of its connection to something deeper unseen but simply felt or maybe acknowledged.

I look out from the bunkers crows nest the exhaust of the air conditioner roars and merges with the dog barks below climbing up from the dog park as Hélène's humming through a piece classical I feel it as silence.

I think perhaps somewhere I acknowledge it as something louder than sound more noticeable than noise, silence.

This is where I have been carried in my 61st year.

I am only that - really I am.

Life continues to be hard the last year and a half have been what i have declared the hardest years of my life all matters of weapons have been used against my humanity and emotionally, physically and right to my very soul.

No one has new unexpected surprises for me that I admittedly fear.

Still I rage against that I rage against the hardship of life with tears in my eyes and feet as firmly planted in the ground to take on the hard battles ahead.

This is not a whine or a sorrowful lament on life as it may be.

It is the acknowledgement of the fuckedupness of being a human being day to day and the madness of will that we carry on accomplishing more than we thought possible at any given moment.

Whether it be in a smile a created meal a good day's work or a moment of love shared with ourselves or someone or something else.

glass beads

The morning presents itself
As a new day

Each new day is holy
Or an unholy glass bead
Strung on a piece of time
a clear piece of fishing wire

Day after Day day after day
Side by side

The holy cheek to cheek
With the unholy
Weighing in on
The piece of wire

Until the weight of days
Bears down and snaps

Time in two.

The beads tumble and come
To rest in rest waiting
Holy scattered next to unholy
They transform neither holy or unholy

Simply glass beads just beads
To be restrung one at a time
In time at another time

The Scar

sitting here my emotions beaten numb
staring into the florescent lights
rather than down the hall
better to see the light than
faces around me reflecting my fright

she is alone   away from me
I am alone   away from her
away from her   down   down
down

the hall   a hall
I move my hand up and finger
an ancient scar
above
my eye
and jesus   I remember the scar

but not how   we put it there

when did we move so close
to the end
and so far   from the start

not surprised   just didn't notice

**tranny chaser one
'fencing'**

On the days when it's fencing day, where everybody gets together in front of the Wellesley confectionery, across from the wine store. Not too long ago the guy who has run that store for years got attacked in the head with a screwdriver.

They get together in front of the convenience store to compare what they have and where it's going to be fenced. They brag about fire hydrants…whatever they've stolen, ice, laundry hampers. Fencing, it's when someone steals stuff and sells it to someone else who will sell it again for more. The stories are larger than the imagined items stolen and bragged about. These stories are the real collateral rather than the loot.

When they all get together in their group meeting, usually they all have bicycles, stolen bicycles of course. As I'm walking home from work around 6pm I can see them all buzzing about their shit, just buzzing back and forth doing whatever they do. As I approach I can see this one guy about six foot two, and he's buzzing with everybody and he catches me coming. I can see the recognition so I don't make eye contact. This happens every couple of weeks. He waits till I get about the length of an apartment building away from him and then he comes up to me and says, "You want to smoke a joint?" Then when he gets that I'm not into it and he says, "What's your name?" I say "It doesn't matter and there is nothing left. I don't have anything left that is attracting you in the first place. That's all gone."

He looks shocked and he says "I just wanted to know if you wanted to smoke a joint." Then he says "do you know if there's any more girls around who might want to smoke a joint."

This happens with the exact same guy every couple of weeks for about two years. He would definitely address my 'trans -ness" as part of the allure. He's chasing me, tranny chasing. So I just tell him again, "Well you're doing the wrong chasing with the wrong person."

Once it ended I knew that I would have far less attention. Tranny chasing attention perhaps but attention is attention. He was not a bad looking man.

He once said "I like to date girls like you. Would you like to smoke a joint?" I'd say no and he'd say, "Would you like to have some sex." I'd just say "I ain't got none of the shit you need for us to have sex" - dawning on him that all the things he would have loved about me were in different places than he could have imagined."

I never told him I had my surgery. I just knew he would understand as soon as I said "Everything that you want and need from me isn't there." I addressed him as "dude." I knew what he wanted, I could tell the minute he spotted me, like clockwork. He has no idea what I have but he thinks he does, the same thing, week after week. But I don't have anything he wants. That's all gone.

looking glass

It's in the moment
It's in the blur
It's in the feel
We must beware

Time runs fast
It twists and turns and burns
The seconds we call ours
A view of concrete
A scent of a flower

thoughts words ideas

I have many crippled moments
filled by crippled minutes

It's not sleeping in or getting ready
That makes me late
It's the unhinged not quite ready psyche
That keeps me from leaving my bunker

My crippled moments and crippled minutes
And although I have travelled
Between heaven and hell and back
Not once but twice today
I am not asking you to
Breathe for me

Walk for me

Or carry my bags

If you stare straight
Into the sun
You will go blind

If you stare directly
Into your soul
You will either
Go mad or awaken

Be inspired
Live life

tranny chaser two
'it's their eyes'

About ten to fifteen years ago I'm walking down Church Street and this older man is following me for two blocks. He speeds up, passes me, stops in front of me. He was about 20 yrs older than me - in his mid 60s. He says "Hi, how are you?" I thought oh my god, I'm not even standing on the street corner and they are coming at me, another tranny chaser. I can see it in their eyes. There's a lot they have going on that trannies can see a mile away. When they think of what's underneath. "Do you want a date" he says. I think this is so fuckin classic. He says "Where do you work?" I say "No. I'm good. I'm nothin that yer looking for." He says "Do you know where I could find some girls like you." I was in a bad mood that day and said "what do you mean girls like me?" If he just called me tranny, but he can't bear to, he doesn't want to admit to that. He wouldn't use that word himself. So he says, "You know, girls like you, you know what I mean." I say "There's a bar over on queen west. Ask around, you'll find it." There wasn't really a bar. I said it to get rid of him. He's probably still looking for a girl like me, still stuck in the loop.

Cleansing

Skeletons of the sea take a new place
Glistening with a new beauty
A gift of the sea to the land
A talisman of wonder
A spell of nature
A spell to maroon madness
The madness of ""moloch"
The madness of isolation
The madness of fear and doubt
Return return to the sea
The cleansing has begun

'cervix buster'

It was over thirty years ago. Our first date was at the Capitol Theatre in Windsor to see Air Farce. I saved that theatre, as the executive director of the Windsor Arts Council. Saved it. And then they fired me. Said I stole money cuz they couldn't find receipts, found the receipts three years later but no apology and I was gone. I heard it all secondhand, they said someone like me couldn't work there, and that I'd never work in that city again.

But on that first date, at the Capitol, I had just got my new toy. My date was a well off guy with a big warehouse space overlooking the river toward Detroit - an established well off artist. He was sixty. I was around thirty. He didn't know about my surgery. The first time we had sex, well, he was a little guy about five foot something. He was small but had the biggest dick I'd ever seen in my life. So big.

He said, "Oh my god I've never slept with someone who looks like a Playboy model." That motherfucker went right through my brand new cervix. I went right into the clinic the next day. I couldn't move. I couldn't breathe. I thought I was having an appendix attack, or something leftover from bad surgery. So I'm in the stirrups and the doctor told me that the surgery is so exact even gynaecologists can't tell. He is looking and says "okay you can get dressed now." I'm dressed and still bent over.

At the time I had moved back in with my mother after leaving the girl from my 'coming home' story. She had a new boyfriend, a saxophone player, we lived together for awhile with me on the couch. It didn't work at all. They treated me like shit.

So I get dressed and the doctor comes into the office and has a prescription for me. I say, "What's wrong, what's going on." He had a thick accent. He says, "Oh Miss Wilson. Yer okay but you had too vigorous of sex. Here is some valium. Please take at least an hour before sex so you can relax." I had been so tense i was clenching my cervix and hurting myself."

As I got dressed and walked down the hall I could hear the laughter of the nurses giggling - not tranny giggling, but she's getting laid a lot kind of giggling

But the short guy with the huge dick, he wanted me to move in with him so I felt I had to tell him about being trans. So I told him we had to meet. Turns out he expected it to be about having a child out of wedlock and the child would have to move in, which he said was okay with him. But he didn't know what to do with what I actually told him. So he went to the priest who ran the AA centre and talked to him about it and told the whole story to the priest. The priest said to him that he had been given a rare gift and that he should go for it. But he ran. He said to me, "I can't be with you anymore because the thought that you once had a dick is too much for me." Ironic when his dick was too much for me.

I used to have to have sex with him with me on top. I had to be in control. Later I heard that the same thing from a lot of other women in the city.

Suddenly awake

Suddenly I am awake, my eyes thrown open by what was on the other side of them while they were closed. Dreams. Breathing fast I listen to everything around me, waiting, holding my breath now, to make sure the coast is clear, praying a silent prayer to the holy picture above my bed that the demons of sleep have not followed me to my bedroom. Downstairs I hear what sounds like a sound that I know, still, I mindfully can't place it. I get up and run to the stairwell past the darkened open closet door, which I am sure I closed before I went to bed to keep what should stay in the closet in the closet. I run down the enclosed stairwell to the closed door that opens to the kitchen. There is creaking on the other side. I sit down on the stairs and listen so hard my ears are hurting. Then I smell it - a faint smell of steam and detergent perhaps. My mother is awake with me, ironing the clothes alone while the rest of the house sleeps. I know I can't sit there much longer and there is no way I will go back up those stairs to bed, so I take the leap of faith and head out the stairwell door and look up at my mother as she is dampening a shirt and rolling it into a ball before she irons it. She looks at me and shakes her head, "What are you doing up again, it's a school night? I had a bad dream," I say. "You always have bad dreams, you have to stop this." She looks at me and leaves the room and comes back with a big blanket and pillow and puts me in my dad's big chair next to where she is ironing. "Now go to sleep, you have school tomorrow." I respond,

"Tell me a story so I can sleep." "No" she says, pausing for a second, then, "What do you want to hear." "Tell me about when I was born." "Ok then you have to go to sleep." "Ok I will try" - and as I wait for her to start, in my grade school head I am trying to work out a no school day. The story goes on and on and I stay awake until I hear my favourite part. Mom gets to the part I love and she knows it and lowers her voice and looks at me as if this is a spell she is casting on me, for me. Then she says, in the middle of the night, she says almost in a whisper, "You decided it was time to be born. I had to wake your father up and we rushed to the hospital and you kept me up all night until early in the morning when you were born yelling and screaming. That is why I know you will always be a night owl, because you came in the middle of the night and keep me up all night until the sun came up." My favourite part of the story, and perhaps then her prediction and that which became my life long truth.

Maybe ten or more years later I am asleep in a rotting double decker bus that once was the magic bus to adventure. My first night sleeping in Topanga canyon California and I am deep down the rabbit hole, and suddenly my eyes are again thrown open by the sound of hard rain hitting the bus and the awful smell of eucalyptus trees which nearly surround us. I open my senses fully and realize I hear the rain but can't see it on the windows or actually hear it on the roof. Sleep panic attack. Where am I, complete confusion. A moment of fear starts to move through me. I, as I did many years ago, take a leap of faith, and sit up, and look out the window. I am greeted by a huge male horse, it raises its head to look at me as it continues to take the longest biggest piss on the side of the bus which moments ago I was sleeping in. Mystery rainstorm solved.

Route 66
the real road
the original
I watched for Cassady and Kerouac
In buses cars and in
the eyes of hitchhikers
1976 through America
speeding
on two lanes
America celebrated
the real America
Of course both Cassady and Kerouac
were dead
But the road it
it remembers
it remembers
remembers them
both
and others
as if it
were yesterday
were yesterday
yesterday
America the real America
forgotten
not a memory
and the road and all those
who it remembers
weep for an
America forgotten

Rock and Roll

It lives it's real raunch on a dirty city stoop
blinded by class but sold to slavery

it cries for the loss

Rock and Roll is a screaming body part

or "the boy in the hallway."

A shattered simplistic corpse in the wrong hands

Rock and Roll

is the dusty summer parched trailer park

It lives it's real raunch on a dirty city stoop.
A dream of freedom on the run
A gash of light in a bleak darkness of despair

Rock and Roll   Rock and Roll
We weep with you and in the trailer park

on the city stoop

A generation a new generation is calling for you and on you to make them move.

Coming Home - one

I only accepted the invitation to read in the city of my birth because it created a reason for me to be there. I would never go there for a visit as it held many emotional issues for me from having it be the home town of my deceased parents who I still love and miss daily and it made some emotional scars itch when I came into town and saw the ragged landmarks that were visible from the road or the train car.

I did not intend to contact anyone from my past while I was here other than those that would be of the sort to come to the reading if they knew about it. My only family left here was a sibling. My younger brother now retired at 60 from the post office and settled into his place as a retired white small city homophobic, transphobic and close-minded male. His last birthday I did not even call him, although he was always nice to me, I couldn't bear his putting who I truly am out of his mind, to talk to me to the point where he still used after thirty something years the pronoun I was born into and I worked so hard to change. A dickhead. Blood is blood but a dickhead is a fucking dickhead.

Anyway I had a day and half before the reading to myself and I decided to go to some places I had frequented as a teenager or maybe as a young adult. I was drawn to my area in the city where I had spent my youth from grade one till I left home at 17 and then returned to for another few years while my father died an awful death from liver cancer finally pushing the place away by 1977.

There was a park - walking distance to my home then - I frequented often, since the time I was allowed free access to the world. Four or five blocks away, it was separated into two parts by what seemed back then like a huge overpass that rose over the train tracks that carried everything industrial in and out of the city. The one side closest to my home was the picnic area and the children's play area with the usual now declared unsafe wading pool, monkey bars and assorted teeter totters, death swings etc. The other side was the interesting part as it contained for me the most beautiful gardens with a fountain containing fish and lilies and thousands of wishing pennies at the bottom. This was of course before lotteries and legal gambling so the unreachable dreams were somehow tied to copper coins wished upon and thrown into the fountain.

This was the park where I sat with my first love, holding incense while guitars played and people sang and talked of the war in Vietnam and other abuses to the world. We were going to change it with love and peace as Woodstock had happened and made us believe it was possible.

This was before The Rolling Stones and The Altamont Speedway concert ended the love generation in 69 and the innocence of a time. I was youngish, maybe all of 14 at these love ins, and truth be told I only attended because an older girl I knew who was so hippy beautiful was afraid to go on her own and had asked me to go with her.

There were many things about the park I loved. There was only one warning I ever received about it, which I never understood until I had to go against the warning - "Stay out of the parks public washrooms." It took one visit to know I was not in the need for the extra curricular events that happened in there, and truthfully, did not completely comprehend, it just wasn't my place to pee.

One of my favourite things in the park was the Boer War Memorial next to the gardens and the fountain. It was a work of art to me. It was a bone white stone, an almost single piece memorial that could have come out of a Joseph Conrad novel. Names and information and sculptures were carved into it alongside brass plaques, it felt as if it was from another world and time. There was a place to sit built into a place to muse over the gardens and hear the water trickle. At least this is how I remembered it and was curious to see if my memories were firing or I had fallen on hard times in the youthful recollections department. I spent many hours as a child and as an adult there just sitting and thinking and sometimes reading a book or two. I remember reading Naked Lunch by William Burroughs there as an eighth grader and not fully understanding everything I was reading or picturing in my mind.

So, since I had time to kill, I ventured to the park to see the gardens and my place of so much youthful thought and perceived beauty associated with that oh so innocent time. Of course how innocent was my time if I had started to read Burroughs's Naked Lunch? Never mind, onward.

The sculpture was still there in the middle of the pond and the gardens seemed smaller in some areas and larger in others. I walked around the water and looked for the fish, there were none, and I could see the stroking of time taking its toll on the things around me just as it has on me. Still, I was glad to be there and headed to my Boer War Memorial, and suddenly realizing I had forgotten that Robert Burns had a statue and tribute to him there too. I passed a man perhaps around my age maybe younger hard for me to tell these days, he had long grey hair, well kept, well dressed, and he walked with a spring in his step that immediately endeared him to me. We made eye contact as we passed, and then I heard the crunch of the small white stones that were under foot surrounding the water garden being ground under his shoe as he must have spun around to call after me. "Hello, are you Patricia Wilson?" I stopped and immediately had a panic thought, could this be someone who I knew from when I worked for a couple of the arts organizations here, just before I met my girlfriend of 25 years and moved the fuck out of there to my beloved Toronto. I did not want to really run into anyone that wasn't part of the plan for this visit. I turned and said yes I am she and he approached me with his hand out to shake mine and said he had read my work. "Thank you" I said, with a quiet breath of relief, "I always wanted to know who the one person was that had read it." He was taken aback, then smiled and moved into a dialogue to tell me how much he loved what I had written. "Thank you so much for sharing this with me, it means a lot to me" I said, and started to walk away towards my destination in the park. "Could I be bold, and make a strange request?" he said. I turned to face him holding my breath for what was to come. "Could you meet my wife, we are within walking distance to the church service she is at right now."

"I, I don't think that's possible, as I have a schedule and limited time to see the park" I said. Thinking to myself, what the fuck, "come meet my wife" at a church service? Thoughts of religious zealots, Amway, Tupperware parties, Mary Kay Makeup requests all slammed into my brain at the same time.

"I know it sounds goddamn crazy, but I am not. I have told her about your writing and I may never get this opportunity again to have her meet you. She has been so resistant to reading your book that I thought if she met you, she might jump in." Wtf I thought this is getting more and more strange. I actually looked around to see if there was a film crew around, in case I had walked into some local cable channels idea of candid camera. One thing caught me like a fucking fish on a lure, the sentence he threw at me when he said,-"She has been so resistant to reading your work that I thought if she met you, she might jump in."

"Ah, she doesn't want to read my work?" I said. Now my ego became the reel and was pulling me in towards the boat far faster and stronger than my ability to fight being hooked with strength of common sense and self-preservation. "No, it is so weird, she loves to read writing similar to yours and I would have thought she would have loved it?"

"Well," I said in a whisper. I am now at this point in the fucking net on my way to be skewered and roasted over an open fire, and someone's fucking dinner. "How far is it?" I ask. Immediately I react by throwing my hand over my mouth to stop any more stupid from coming out of it. Shit, too late by the telling look on his face. He smiles and points in a direction over my shoulder. "Not far at all you can see the steeple from here." I turn around and see a small, gray'ish, steeple at the end of his point that I don't remember being there while I lived here. Do they still build churches, and with steeples? Strange. I don't see any pentagrams or flashing lights or entities spinning around it. I think to myself, I can always bolt suddenly and head in another direction if the fucking doors bolt open and hundreds of cult members come rushing out en masse like deadly army ants to grab a new member. So, without uttering a word, I turn around, and start down the path out of the park towards the destination of doubt. He quickly gets what I have decided and pulls up beside me and we walk silently for a few yards. "I'm Stanley," he offers to me. I stop and turn to face him slightly embarrassed that I had been so self involved, I had forgotten to ask him his name. "Oh I am so sorry I forgot to ask you your name" I say, in a weak voice. "Not a problem or a worry, there was a lot going on back there," Stanley kindly offers to me.

I can't help but like this man, he seems kind, aware, and full of life or something akin to wonderment. At the same time I realize I am coming to this conclusion about him, after what, 10 or 15 minutes at the most of conversation. I immediately get so distracted that I stumble over a curb and as I stumble he quickly grabs my arm to steady me and asks, "You ok?" "Yes, yes," I say, "Just not watching where I am going, thank you for helping me there." He has strong steady hands I think to myself as we continue down the path. "I wonder if there is something else happening here?" I say in a low, meant only for me, mumble. " Excuse me? Stanley says, "I missed that, with all the traffic noise and such." I say - "Just talking to myself, something I do more and more these days." He responds with, " I get that, I am completely guilty of that too."

Stanley is right, there is a lot of traffic as we pull up to the corner just outside of the park. "Christ, I don't remember it ever being this busy when I lived here," I say in a voice tinged with angry surprise. "Yes, although things are definitely not at their productive best these days, the traffic has grown and taken over parts of the city," he offers. As we stand there waiting for the lights to change I subconsciously reach over and touch my phone in my right hand breast pocket of my jean jacket making sure it's there and suddenly thinking, I may need it, depending on what happens in the next little while. I look around to the four corners and not a damn thing on any corner looks or feels the same as it did so many years ago. Can things change so fast? I mean literally not one thing here in front of me presents even a shadow of a memory.

Surprisingly too, is that there is no life, no human activity on any of the corners to warrant such a destruction of what was once there. A four cornered ghost town. My stomach is now starting to take the hit of all this and I can feel myself growing more and more uncomfortable. Now as we walk silently towards the building he calls the church, I can barely concentrate on anything except the growing discomfort in my stomach. I can't take this kind of thing anymore, I think to myself. How did I let this happen, I mean going against my better judgment and walking wide eyed into this. Fuck. Too late now the only thing on my mind is finding a washroom so I can relieve the growing pain in my stomach and bowels.

Now I am saying a prayer myself, as I walk up the stone steps of the church towards the door, "Please God let me get to the can before I shit myself." As we enter the sunlit foyer I turn to Stanley, trying to look calm, and say to him in what I hope is in a calm steady voice, "Where is the washroom?" He politely points in the direction of the stairs leading to the basement and says, "Down the stairs straight ahead and to the right." I sigh and excuse myself and walk at a measured pace towards my goal. As I open the door to the single toilet washroom I silently thank the bathroom gods for the opportunity to do my deed in privacy.

I literally explode, all the tension and doubt of this escapade being thrown out of me and I immediately start to come to myself again. "No mess to clean up, thank God," I think to myself, and after looking in the mirror to make sure all is where it should be I head back up to where I left Stanley minutes ago.

"Hey," I say as I approach him, slightly startled at the casualness of my greeting as I usually throw that salutation towards old friends rather than new untested acquaintances. "Hey back" he says, picking up on the change in my demeanour. I think, "Don't get too relaxed with me, you fucker, one false move and I will make your head spin."

So we slide through the doors into the main worship room and I suddenly take a short gasp of air. I look up and see the room lit by the sunlight broken up into a thousand rays of light by the refraction of the sun beams interpreted through the red purple coloured glass skylights. Mixed with the effect of the sunlight are the lights of hundreds of hanging candles in metal cages. Once my eyes adjust to the lights and the effects, I saw and then heard the few cages with couples of songbirds singing happily to each other and everyone that would listen.

Needless to say the unexpected beauty of light mingled with the sound of the birds was, I don't know how to describe it correctly, but I was moved to almost tears. Stanley was studying my face and obviously was familiar with the reactions of those experiencing this for the first time, so he said to me simply. "Beautiful, isn't it? It helps lead one to one's self, one's path." I continued to stare upward and then scanned the whole room. The room was simple with a few found pews from other churches, a few mats, some chairs and cushions on the floor, and a few steps on the south side of the room that led to a candle lit and incense covered altar-like structure. Not really an altar in the true sense of the word, it felt as though it was more of a centrepiece for the room. There were the idols of course - the Buddhas, the stars, the crucifixes and many items I could not make out in the light and my distance from the 'altar' - a worship room for all.

I feel Stanley touch my hand softly to get my attention and he slightly leans into me and in a whisper he said, "I would like you to meet my Mary." The way he said it sounded so loving and endearing I felt a little weak kneed. He raised his hand in the direction of a woman who was sitting in one of the old found church pews and we walked noiselessly towards her. As we came up beside her I knew something was about to happen. I felt I was going to faint or maybe even vomit and I began to shake. He put his hand on her shoulder and said "Mary, this is Patricia Wilson, the woman whose writing I have been asking you to read."

She hesitated a bit too long before standing and turning towards me, with her trembling hand outstretched she raised her eyes to meet mine. It was Mary, once my Mary, and I was once hers too. We had not seen or spoken to each other in over thirty years and we had not walked away from each other unscathed. Mary was my partner when I started my transition so long ago. Suddenly being face to face with her and the flooding memories, I found I could barely breathe, and I felt my chest go tight, and by the looks of it she was doing no better than I was. We both instinctively sat down not saying a word to each other or to Stanley. He looked at us both and in a shaky voice he said, "Is, is, everything alright? What's going on?" It was well known in certain circles that both Mary and I had 'travelled' - in that she pretty well fucking hated me.

It was never really her fault considering how long ago it was and how little information there was available to anyone really when it came to transsexuality. The information around then was one step above a back page story in the Readers Digest. I know because I read that back page story and read about something that vaguely was me, although a line in the fucking story about 'suicide and the victims' affected by this mental illness shocked and terrified me. The strange thing is that although someone that is "fluid" (as they say now) has a battle in front of them, it's the ones that love them and they love that get damaged terribly too. Your search to be who you truly are destroys a part of them that they loved and cherished about you. So, your family, lovers and friends must climb that sadness and confusion to find the thing that they loved and cherished in a different package, sort of. I'm not saying that love and understanding won't eventually come to the whole thing, but if you're not personally aware of what it feels like, and the self damage and sometimes self hate that it brings, you can't understand it. Like Renée Richards said in her book many years ago, I am paraphrasing here, "It is hard for a free fish to understand what a caught fish feels like." That one line stuck with me my whole life my whole zigzag journey.

Although Mary knew from the day we met as I was upfront with her and she started out as my confidante - we fell into a precarious love. I think both hoping that this weird cup I would not have to drink deeply from.

Still I knew deep down in my soul where it would go as I had given up love, true love, already, and had given my gender roller coaster, honestly, as the reason for the complete destruction of that relationship.

Looking back I realize for me when I finally started to transition, and it was an up and down, back and forth, stopping hormones starting hormones, heartbreaking and joyful, all depending on the moment, or the hour, or the day, or who I thought I was in love with then. I know now that although I was transitioning to be who I knew I was, I lost who I was psychically and emotionally for years, because of the struggle in front of me. I battled those around me, family, friends, gas station attendants, grocery store clerks, pointing laughing strangers, whispering bar patrons, driving me into a deep depression and an intense agoraphobia that prevented me from moving forward in many ways.

Mary and I were living together then and she endured and lovingly helped me stumble through it all until I got my first job in the arts as the woman who I was learning and growing to be. We stayed together until shortly after my surgery, which ultimately broke her heart and mine, for lost love is always heartbreaking no matter what the reason, good or bad. By that time I was sleeping on the couch while she slept in what was once our bed with a man that would be part of her life for a minute. It was so strange and new for me and I sobbed and cried alone many nights, even though I had the joy of my surgery and a life that I was beginning to understand and love. We eventually had a complete falling out after I had moved out and she had a huge back yard ceremonial bonfire of all my books and things that I had left behind at her house. I wonder if she had someone sage her house too. I probably would have.

Now after a million breaths and her few thousand silently screamed fuck yous, here we were face to face. Neither one of us ever wanted to or expected to look each other in the eyes again. The thing was, as this catastrophic meeting began to unfold, one of the very first things that crossed my mind was, "I am going to write about this." And here it is true to my word.

I wonder if I have warped the meeting as the emotion and the hate and disgust thrown at me with cutting eyes may have been too much to write clearly about. I remember seeing all that in her eyes - like a hissing cobra as she said, "Why are you here?" Before I could answer Stanley said - "I…I brought her here. I met her in the park and thought you two could talk and…"…"Enough" she almost gasps. "Get out" she says in a whisper so those around her can't hear her hateful or brokenhearted command.

Sometimes broken hearts disguise themselves as hateful hearts. I wanted to take Mary's hand. I wanted to explain to her all she did not know of me since that time and why things happened. I even wanted to apologize to her for her pain and bitterness and tell her that she is better than this. So, taking a steady breath I took her quivering hand and leaned into her, slightly intimate as two long time friends would do, and I said quietly to her, "Go fuck yourself." I dropped her hand, grabbed Stanley's and said, "Thank you, I hope her nightmares don't become yours" and I walked out of the church feeling better than I had in a very long time.

Crow *for Hélène*

Caw Caw Caw
My my my
Girl girl girl
Is a black feathered
Crow

She swoops and calls
The faithful to her breast
To collect their shiny words

Words so bright
Words so bright
Collecting heavens words
Shiny shiny

they are the wind for her wings
What is shiny and bright
Worth the work to carry
To her for her

Seems dull and uninteresting
To me to me
It is the magic
Her magic

A thought
A word
A bottle
A piece of cloth

Shine with the magic
Her magic
A magic not mine
Still
Importantly
I am the witness
The other side

I am the glint
of the shine
In her eye

Remember
A crow and
It's voice
It's voice
It's voice

It's the twist
Of the magic
A shiny musical
Spell.

Breathe

We breathe your empty dreams
We watch your empty symbols
Our muted shouts for enlightened glory
frozen in the dirty burning air
Secular secular will not save
A rumbling of salvation aligns itself
With the screaming locomotive of despair
A Trojan horse for the soul
A Trojan horse of the soul
Salvation a seed of growing light
Unseen till it breaks the surface
In the face of screaming despair
In the face screaming despair
Salvation from deep below

Coming Home - two

As I was leaving the church and began walking down the steps I realized I was light headed and at the same time my ears felt as though they were straining to hear some reaction to the "go fuck yourself" that I had given Mary as a reunion present. For a millisecond I wanted to stop dead in my tracks and wait, and I didn't even know what I wanted to wait for or what I expected. I said out loud, without thinking, "now the story begins." I was so deep in my head and with my knees shaking I almost missed the last step and I stumbled slightly and as I fought to regain my balance a strong arm grabbed me by the elbow and helped steady me. I turned around quickly to see who had grabbed - well not grabbed but who had steadied me in my recovery, and fucking shit it was Stanley. I hadn't heard or had seen him come up behind me. "You alright?" He asked in a steady voice almost as if he hadn't witnessed the meeting in the church. My emotions raced from anger to astonishment maybe even a tinge of pure joy when I saw him. I looked him in the eye and said maybe a bit too forcibly, "I am not sorry, I have no guilt, I want you to understand that." He stood not speaking for a moment and his eyes searched my face and he took in a quivering breath and said to me "I know, I know, nor should you." I suddenly felt angry that he was there and I needed to get the hell away from him, the church, my memories and I turned around without a word and started walking down the sidewalk in the wrong direction and I heard his voice clearly above the bus that was roaring past me, "You're headed the wrong way." Almost to spite him I continued a few more steps in the wrong direction, then I stopped and I was surprised to feel hot tears running down my cool cheeks. "Oh no," I whispered out loud to myself, "Not fucking now, wait, wait."

I did not want Stanley to see this and I didn't want to share anything more with him or with this fucking city for that matter. Right that moment I wasn't happy with who I was or who I could have been. I needed to sit down and have a big fucking drink. So I turned around and started to walk back from where I had just come from and I kept my head down and away from Stanley but I raised my head just a few steps away from him and looked directly at him and continued on my way down the street with the idea I could perhaps find a little place to have a drink and decompress. Walking for about five minutes I saw the flashing Coors light and Budweiser signs just ahead of me on my left. A somewhat little bar with a weird fake wooden façade and maybe a six table front patio. I slowed down as I approached the place, looked inside and saw that it was empty except for a couple of people and the bartender. I looked around for the name of the joint and saw the obviously hand painted marquee that proclaimed I was entering Jan's Pub. Fine, quiet and easy to just disappear into one of the little booths across from the bar on the opposite wall. I went over to the bartender and asked for a double Jack Daniels and soda on ice short and she looked at me and started to frown. "Oh I am so sorry we don't have Jack Daniels here, maybe a bourbon or a Jameson instead?" "Oh fuck," I said to myself, "Can this be true?" I just walked into probably the only bar in this city that doesn't have Jack Daniels." Fucking figures this is my day all wrapped up in a sentence.

"Oh!" I said lowering my voice for some reason "No just give me a house draft and a double shot of tequila in a glass on the side with the lime or lemon however you do it here, and please bring me the bill at the same time." She paused for a second and looked at me and I felt she was about to say something but either thought better of it or it was not important. Ok by me, I was happy not to have to talk anymore than I had to. Still she turned away from pouring the draft to look up and say "Go sit down and I will bring you your drinks." I nodded my head and turned around eyeing the booth as though it was a sanctuary for lost souls and slid into it surprised on how small it actually was. As I looked around and got comfortable, a thought crossed my mind that I must have passed this place on the way to the church but missed seeing it somehow. After being a bartender for so long I usually automatically sense or see bars in close proximity to me. Well maybe the stress and weirdness of the whole thing fucked up my powers of observation. I smiled and said out loud to myself "I wonder if I missed anything else?" "Pardon me?" I heard next to me, the bartender was standing there about to coaster my drinks in front of me and I hadn't seen her arrive. "Oh shit," I said looking at her, "sorry, I was actually talking to myself" "That's ok" she said all perky like "I do it all the time and I even answer myself" she finished the sentence with a beatific smile.

She finished placing my drinks on the Coors Light coasters and I thanked her and she turned and headed to the bar where a new customer had just plopped down on the barstool. I fumbled with the lemon on the edge of my glass and downed the tequila letting it burn before I sucked on the lemon and took a long drink from my glass of beer. I heard myself sigh and suddenly self conscious that I had sighed too loud I glanced over towards the bar to see if anyone had heard me. Nope, thank god, as I reached into my jacket pocket to answer my vibrating telephone. It was my host here in the city, wanting to know what was happening. As I concentrated on texting out help messages to my host, I felt a presence at the end of the booth hovering quietly but intently. I finished texting my message (or as I call it, tex mexing), which included my whereabouts and how I was in immediate danger of many things including losing my shit. I put my phone down, perhaps a bit too loudly, and there she was, the bartender, standing there at the end of the booth with two glasses of what I assumed to be tequila because of the lemon on the rim. "Thought you looked like you could use another shot," she smiled, "and because it's bad luck to do one on your own, I am going to join you." :Oh, cool" I said. "Thank you, it's not necessary, but I will be happy to knock this back with you right now." I of course thought for a second, did I fuck my luck up a minute ago doing the other shot on my own? No matter this is cool and obviously it is way better tequila than I had downed on my lonesome a few minutes ago. She raised our two shot glasses she had grabbed in her one hand towards me as a sort of empty glass that was a cool kind of salute. Of course I knew the language. I had done the same thing thousands of times over the years when I had been behind the bar. I sipped the rest of my beer, and in what was perfect timing my phone vibrated and it was my ride outside waiting for me.

I got up with my bill and my cash in hand only to find the bartender at the end of the booth again. I must have looked startled because she said, "Oh sorry, I came to see if you need the machine or change for your bill." "No, it's cool." I said. Noticing she didn't step back as I stood up to slide out of the booth, so when I was standing up I was way too close and could smell her perfume mixed with a slight scent of hard liquor. The sexiest perfume in the world in my opinion, perfume mixed with the smell of hard liquor. I actually had to place my hand on her arm to get by her. I said "Thanks again for the shot it was delicious" and she said, "It was wasn't it?" I headed for the door and just before I reached the door I heard her from behind me softly yell, "I will see you at your reading tonight."

Consider me a fish caught hook line and sinker. I was gobsmacked. I opened the door out to the street and surprisingly, there was still enough daylight left so I could put my sunglasses on legitimately, although lack of sun had never stopped me before.

MUSINGS FROM
THE BUNKER 2017/19

March 26 at 1:07 PM

So many books to read so little time in my mind to do it. Hélène is heading out to walk the dogs and I am finishing my coffee and getting ready to hit the office at the theatre. Not much to say today but will leave you with a quote that caught my eye this morning.

"Do notice: We still counted happiness and health and love and luck and beautiful children as "ordinary blessings."

Blue Nights by Joan Didion

March 25 at 1:13 PM
Today is March 25th and my mothers birthday. She would have been 98 today. She was all she could be and everything to me. The first picture was her beginning her career as a Bell Canada Supervisor and the other was a head shot she had taken in Detroit. My mother waited to marry till her mid 30s which was quite an unusual thing to do back in those days. I bought flowers for her today her favourite, carnations. She wrote journals and was a gifted letter writer. My sister the keeper of family keepsakes sent me one of her hardcover journals that she never got a chance to write in. So I will use it for those special moments. We are always together in love and kindness. Happy birthday mom I love you. Be kind today, love is the answer. Peace.

March 25
Sitting by the computer watching Velvet Underground docs and interviews with Joan Didion, David Bowie and Patti Smith. An easy glide into my two days off before I do some work on my writing. Thinking of those I love here and beyond. Celebrating them and myself with a beer and a good tequila. Happy Sunday, celebrate love wherever you find it. Be kind and Peace.

March 24 at 3:56 PM

Day off.....So Hélène is out with the dogs in the park blowing the stink off all of them. Had a snack of a tiny piece of toast and olive oil and some coffee. Now I am waiting for the old lady to come home and make us some breakfast while I continue to relax after a busy successful weekend behind the bar at Buddies. Baking a chicken for dinner for all those here in the bunker to enjoy and then making broth tomorrow for the freezer. Today was a memory filled morning chat with Mom and others who have passed on. A few laughs a few wonderfully sweet memories and the odd pang of sadness of loss. Still a good way to start two days off and to finish some editing. Right this minute I am taking a break from watching this and continue to sip a little tequila and a side of beer. Have a good day, enjoy a vice or two today and talk to those who love you whether on this side or the other Be kind and Peace.

March 19 at 10:26 AM

Tuesday morning and it's one of my busiest days of the week. Although I have made time tonight so I could attend the theatre with Dr. Bateman to see Unsafe at Canadian Stage. A rare thing to do for me. Having my morning coffee and going over my manuscript which my editor mentioned above, David Bateman, has put together for me. It's a hard thing to do because it's a tedious task and some of the stories and FB posts and prose contained within still cause some emotional response within me. Oh well that said I just found that Hélène and I are reading the same book at the same time because we have both bookmarked it in different places. A wonder that is, really, that we are so different but have partially grown into each other over the years that this sharing of a book represents to me. Today I found one on Hélène's many lists. She writes lists for everything, she loves list. She makes lists for groceries, operas she wants to listen to, things she needs to do and even sometimes a list on how and what she is feeling about someone or something. The lists are everywhere, on post it notes and notebook paper, just everywhere. Other than the phrase "I love you" over the past 25 something years together the other phrase "make a list" is a very close second to the most said thing directed to me by her. Well a bit more coffee and the spin into the day outside of the bunker will truly begin. Today, follow Hélène's lead and make a few lists and especially one that lists how you love yourself and those around you. Be kind and Peace.

March 17 at 3:53 PM

So it's my day off and Hélène Ducharme, as she does, has entered the world outside of the bunker to satisfy my need for cooking ingredients.

Sadly as she becomes the huntress I become the sloth and am sitting in front of a screen sipping a beer and a side of Old Granddad Bourbon. To make up for being a sinner I am sharing a saint with you here. In case you need a holy fix here it is supplied by Patti Smith [performing The Tiger by William Blake]

March 15 at 9:39 AM

A morning here in the bunker calm surrounded by cat grass, cat toys, books and my coffee. Love is working its spell here and I am thankful. Not so in Christchurch, New Zealand where hate has killed many. Bob Dylan sang it years ago with this. I mourn those who gathered in love of God and each other.

How many deaths will it take till he knows
too many people have died
The answer, my friend, is blowing in the wind
The answer is blowing in the wind...

March 14 at 8:25 AM

…Gibson resting on the grass at Queens Park during a summer walk with us. I am looking forward to the summer and all activities that present themselves this year. Most excited about open windows and our balcony and the flowers. Soon we will celebrate our precious lives outdoors under the sun and warmth. Till then even our memories and day dreams are in the moment and help build the day and calm the heart and soul. Be kind to your daydreams they give you strength. Love is the answer and Peace.

March 13 at 6:48 AM

My morning view as I start my day with my coffee and candles of thanks and thoughts of those who have moved on to another dimension. Not a fan of early daylight as I miss being surrounded with the comforting early morning darkness. So when I can I get up for the chance to read and daydream and write within this cocoon of darkness before it breaks into the light of another day. Of course 4:30am ventures are not possible when scheduled shifts and my days end early mornings after 1am. The next couple days are just daylight shifts so it's good. Realized already today or relearned that to gain knowledge to studiously turn it over and examine it we must drop first our tight assed ego and secondly remain calm that we will benefit from the knowledge as it steps over our discarded dazed ego lying there on the ground in front of us and knowledge wraps its arms around us shining new light into us. More coffee, and back to my work with my pen. Enjoy the light of new knowledge, be kind. Peace.

March 11 at 7:30 AM

Some nights when all the gods and saints and demons have forgotten or missed you and you have just enough alcohol or are high enough that the warmth of being truly human is so wonderful and fulfilling that you can choose to sleep wonderful dreams or choose to stay awake and see where it will take you the choice is a moment and thought away. Tonight with the stepping stone of daylight savings time and a side of Jack Daniels I am awake and waiting to see where will it will take me right this blessed moment. The warmth of being human and all it is surrounds me tonight and I feel as though I can take it and look at it all in slow motion. Be kind to yourself and Peace.

March 10 at 1:38 AM

So today was a long day at the office and behind the bar. I started at 1pm and I'm still here at the theatre working at 12:30am. My feet are sore but damn it what a place to make them work till they hurt. I had a few quiet moments this morning and I really felt that at the end of a day it's the small precious little things that add up up for me to make a fully focused and good day. Not always a day of enlightenment but one of satisfaction that I made it through and had some smiles and laughs along with the head shaking and the wtf's. Here is some eye candy from my work night tonight. Be kind celebrate the small things and Peace

March 7 at 5:15 PM

…my blanket of course covered in cat hair that I have wrapped around me as I sit here and drink my hot coffee. I awoke later than usual cranky and groggy as I was desperate for a full night sleep and had a few Jack shots and a couple of Gravol before going to bed. Obviously bad drug management. Anyway reading The White Album by Joan Didion what a pleasure that is while under a blanket drinking hot coffee. Heading to work soon for a bit of paperwork and a bar shift. Heard or felt my mom say "Snap out of it get it going" so I will listen to her and get going. God bless your mom's, even after they have left us their still helping us along. Be kind and Peace.

March 5 at 3:30 PM

Today March 5 is Hélène's birthday. She has always been a joy within my world and a joy to many others. She sings as you'd expect angels to, with a voice of sweetness, true emotion and pure spirit. She loves life and all things within that life. After over 25 years together I am still learning new things from her and about her. A vibrant, kind and honest human being. Happy Birthday Hélène you make the world a better place.

March 5 at 3:47 AM

Happy birthday Hélène my other set of eyes, my steadying hand the one who helps keep the world at bay when needed. She smiles and laughs at all the perfect and maybe not so perfect times. We spend most of our days together beside each other or together while in different rooms. She has that perfect balance that makes that possible. Smart, sometimes too aggravatingly smart, intense and lovingly clear and precise just short of bugging me. Hélène is a pure clear loving soul without any bullshit and I love her and love who she is and love the years we have grown together. To be part of Hélène's life is to be given a gift no matter what part she occupies in your life. Happy Birthday Hélène heavens angels have shared their voices with you and you have shared yours with us. Xo

March 4 at 11:18 PM

Speaking to the Guardian in 2015, Flint lamented the state of modern pop music. "We were dangerous and exciting! But now no one's there who wants to be dangerous. And that's why people are getting force-fed commercial, generic records that are just safe, safe, safe."

        Keith Flint: Prodigy RIP

March 2 at 7:06 PM

This is our bedroom fan above the bed which for my before bar shift nap contains myself, Gibson our dog and Pearl the cat. I am watching the doc Dream ofLlife about Patti Smith on very low volume to help lull me to sleep. In order to rise above mediocracy you must do the same simple thing over and over. Be kind and Peace.

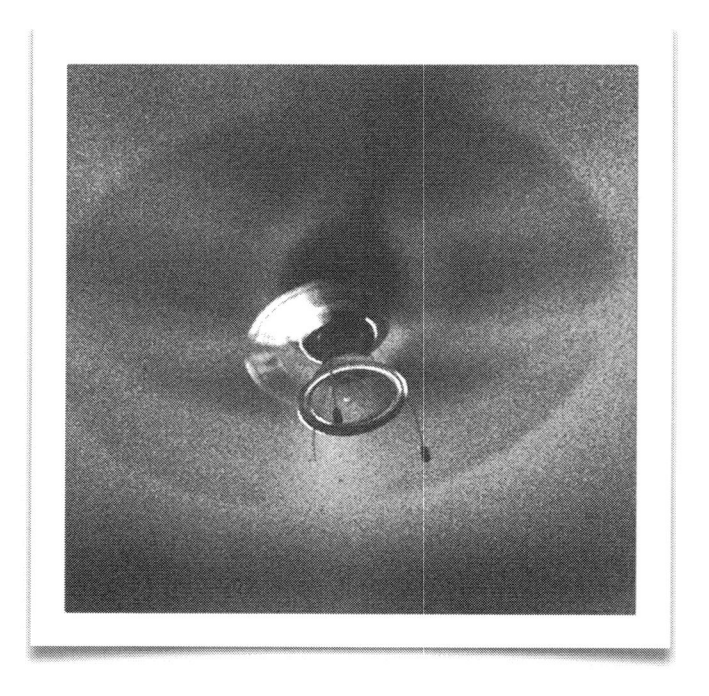

"I absolutely love the rich quotidian detail in your posts. Soothing, and inspiring at the same time."

Judith Thompson

February 26
Having a small piece of sourdough toast with peanut butter and a glass of water as a side as I finish watching the George Harrison doc on Netflix to celebrate his birthday on Feb 25th. Once it is finished it will be time for bed in preparation for hopefully another day to live a good day. Today, oh today, I accomplished no work but I did share some soft and some scary and some lovely moments with Hélène and that will be the colour of today's journey. Be kind, colour your world with the soft, the scary and the lovely moments of companionship. Peace

February 21

So Hélène and I have crawled into bed tonight together true to each other as always, and I realize as we look at each other we still search each other's eyes and every wrinkle on the others face for the answer of who we are to each other and ultimately our very selves. The picture taken here is the end of my night at work and it's all steel and purpose. Our real life at home at night is not that, but the opposite. Not steel but the softness of flesh and of kindness and there is no purpose to our time to shut the night down, just the wonderment and fear and joy of being together at the end of another day. Love is the answer, be kind and Peace.

February 20

Today I am thankful for the mundane, the routine in my life and the uninspired moments around me. They are my salvation and the truth of my humanity and guard against my own madness when it peers at me from its interior window. Love your routine make it your prayer, be kind and Peace.

February 19

Writing about exhaustion as a temporary cure of to much reflection focused on negative or fearful thought. I wrote myself into a panic attack and the ability to move out of it with paper and ink seemed unavailable to me. I realized that my busy weekend and a horribly managed sleep last night has left me exhausted and over tired. It is a blessing as the exhaustion has left me too tired to follow the path that the panic attack was laying out for me. Suddenly, I was steady again because I actually said, "I am too tired to go here now" All that said, I am about to head out to the theatre to do some desk work. It's always a surprise where a human moment can take you. Be kind, struggle, understanding that there is rest from your struggle and Peace.

February 16

Sitting here with Hélène and the cats and dogs, I have stopped writing for the day as even the ink in my pen seemed to lazy to come out and meet the paper. So a coffee and a side of Jack Daniels on ice and intense day dreaming within the wonderful silence around us. Have a day that you can be happy with, be kind, and Peace.

February 15

Writing and studying and marking out interesting passages in books I am inside of at the moment. This one The New Jerusalem by Patti Smith is currently part of my work today. All quiet here in the bunker after a surprising night at the Rhubarb Theatre Festival working behind the bar. Resting my bad knee and using the joint cream to make it ready for another night. Hélène was excited to go off to Koerner Hall at the University of Toronto for a workshop by Jesse Norman the huge opera star who I am sure will say learned and interesting things about music. Back at the bar tonight but another hour of writing if I am lucky. Enjoy the day, be kind chose love first and Peace.

February 14

Happy Valentine's Day. There are many kinds of love and to keep it fresh and strong we must never take any love for granted and re-examine and touch it's heart everyday. Even if only for a vibrating moment. Love is the answer. Be kind, choose love first and Peace.

February 13

…Pearl she is relaxing on my lap as I start my day with my coffee and silent shout outs to those I love and care about both here in this world and in the next one. The next photo is what I see before I start work whether it be writing or reading or getting ready to head to the theatre and my office or to work behind the bar. Inspiration in a flash. Today is the beginning of the two week Rhubarb Theatre Festival so my days will have a few extra hours tagged on to them. Yesterday in a conversation here with a dear friend we talked of our relationships without partners. I tried to sum it up by saying after twenty-something years Hélène is between me and the world and interprets what's out there for me from her point of view and then I filter that with mine. I do the same for her. We are each other's opinion of the world at large which protects us from the worlds cold like a warm blanket in the winter. Be kind. Peace.

February 7

Outside the office door where I shuffle paper and bang on a computer keyboard is a theatre awaiting its talent and audience. It happens next Wednesday for the first week of the Rhubarb festival. So much energy and work and excitement all around the building. The biggest thing though for me is the joy, there is so much joy among the artists and all those involved. The ability to give their work to and for others, how can that produce anything more important than joy. Without joy we become small and dark and lose part of ourselves. Here at Buddies the joy is present. Come to the festival and share your joy as the artists and workers share theirs with all of us. Be kind. Peace.

February 4

Dr. David Bateman sitting at our table here in the bunker enjoying some food and drink after he and I had worked on our collaborative poetry. Tonight we are at it again hammering it out for the future release of our work. Afterwards I will make a simple meal of bangers and mash with the usual alcoholic beverages. Hélène will join us for dinner and we will celebrate the art and the end of a hard week with very sick dogs who are in recovery finally. Life is so full at times and we must chose our moments with our hearts in order not to miss out on what we will cherish in the future about ourselves and those we love. Be kind and Peace.

February 3
So sipping a second Jack Daniels with a whiff of soda while dinner moves into its last stages of cooking. Thinking of the good this week and the shitty and remembering how lucky I am to have people I love and friends that care for me. Of course Hélène Ducharme and the four footers here in the bunker always love me and have my back. Yet in those moments when life feels like it's just too long and shit is all you can step in, friends are the antidote to those emotional times. Celebrate your friends and loves and thank them for all they are. Here is a moment of friendship that happened to me a little while ago. How lucky am I. Be kind and Peace.

January 31
Pirate has taken over my reading chair and I am sipping a little bourbon before our first meal of the day. Writing a poem around this idea that lack of self worth can be a terminal illness to the soul. The world is a hard place, life is hard but what is it that can turn that lack of worthiness around? Love of course but we must really define what true success is to ourselves as human beings not the definition from others or the world at large. We must guide our own ships confidently and take the storms along with the calm seas as just part of the journey. Be kind to yourself and Peace.

January 28

Hélène Ducharme is having an after show cocktail with David Bateman after watching the Met opera at the theatre and I am sipping a very potent Jack and soda and having a ball watching rock videos on our chromecast. It's not intense art going on here but what a fucking fun time i am having right now. Snow, the bunker, drinks, rock and roll and a chance for something new tomorrow. Perfect. Be kind, Peace.

January 28

There are so many spiritual things to be thankful for but not one of them will be as good as a well made Jack and soda.

January 27

…the poetry marathon last night. What a wonderful time we all had and raised money for a queer youth shelter at the same time. I was so honoured to be able to read a few of my new poems. Even if I had to follow the Jimi Hendrix of poetry bill bissett

January 26

So what a great cause at a very important time in this limping city of ours. I took Saturday (tonight) off work to read. Come hear a shit load of poets do their work for the benefit of queer youth. Thanks Shannon Maguire

January 23

Suddenly as I look up the rain has twisted itself into snow. The cats have deserted me out of boredom as I edit and read aloud five or six new poems for Saturday's marathon poetry event at Glad Day Books. The snow has made me feel lighter as I have been feeling anxious over aging in a world where we have little control over so many things. Housing, deep healthcare so many gaps to fall through if your resources are slim. Still we must face the darkness to find the switch that is our light/lightness. People are the light we have the secret to each other's and our own happiness. We are alive and human and despair exists with us but so does love and kindness. Love is the answer. Be kind, don't let fear and despair rob you of the light that is you and those you love. Peace.

January 21

Been up since 5am I was in bed before midnight. The cats are up and hanging with me now as it's after 7 and close to soft food time. Just starting to make broth to freeze and make soup for today. Comfort food on my day off in very wintery conditions. A reading day and some writing although it's not hitting the page easy. Feeling a little off the last couple days but going to ride it out and see where it takes me. We all get to walk that line between heaven and hell daily sometimes more than just once in a day. Being human living my life it's a gift to learn new thoughts and things along with different emotions and sometimes painful to unlearn and revisit and rearrange past thoughts and emotions. I need the down time to do so. Be kind and always ask for help when you can, give someone a chance to share their love. Peace

January 20

A quiet Sunday early evening and I am thinking of starting dinner soon. Hélène is drinking her tea and I am sipping some Rebel Yell bourbon listening to music. This LP [Exile On Main Street, The Rolling Stones] is the soundtrack for our joy of being together and celebrating another day. Be kind and make joy a tool of your daily work. Peace

January 19

… Hélène and myself as seen from the theatre box office point of view taken last summer. Today I woke up with a slight panic because she wasn't next to me. She came and lay down next to me and we talked and cried and laughed over our lives now and our lives together over the quarter of the past century and spoke of our fears and delights ahead of us today and tomorrow and beyond. Intimacy. Life is hard but love is the soft cushion for the soul. Be kind in the present and watch yourself grow. Peace.

January 17

Pirate is enjoying his Brita filtered water that I have just changed along with the four footers food top up and litter (zen garden work) cleaning and all the before bed chores and rituals necessary for a sleep and a start of the day tomorrow. It is 4:35am and I have already slept three or so hours and am now going back to finish the sleep trail. Not a bad day, work wasn't bad, some emotional human stuff, but I and those I love all survived. Hélène and I had a nice quiet dinner of leftovers and were surrounded by the peace of the evening. Today I read and took in new things that I believed were true and at the exact same time I faced what I read as untrue. The glory of growth and learning through the gift from others. Whether we accept their musings as truth and perhaps those musings even feel akin to us, or perhaps, we see those musings as untrue and alien to who we believe at that moment we are. But the truth and the untruth of how we see ourselves changes in a flash. So all things that are about being human whether real or dream are there for us to dissect and build our changes on. Be kind, love the changes that bedazzle you as they will light your way

Peace

January 16

My corner of the office taking a break before I get back to it. Busy week here opening a show tomorrow, a big workshop of Dyke City on Friday and getting ready for the Rhubarb Festival in February. Never mind the dance/club/drag king nights on various Fridays and of course Saturday club. Buddies never a dull moment. Lucky to be working in such a creative hive when I am not writing and creating myself. Today my life feels like it's filled with silver bangles and starry eyed silver skulls. Be kind. Peace.

January 15

6:00am. I was suddenly and widely awake at 3am. So I got up and made some green tea and soaked my slightly infected finger on my left hand. Finished the deed and grabbed my tea to sit down with Pirate the cat and read. I am fully into Murakami's latest release and I am hooked. So I have day work tomorrow at the office In that theatre I work for so I am hoping for a couple more hours of sleep. We will see if the sandman revisits the bunker or not. No matter, insomnia has been both an aggravation and a friend to me at different times over my life. It all depends, sometimes there is just too much to experience to sleep. Or perhaps there is the opportunity for the lack of sleep to create a soothing drug like state that eases the thoughts and can even help with ideas and creativity. Time will tell and life will function today like bird seed scattered randomly on the ground from the birds greedily feeding and arriving in their feeder. Find a secret place for yourself today and enjoy all that is yours. Be kind and Peace.

January 14

Sipping the last of my morning coffee which I have now paired with a little bourbon to carry me along as I spend the afternoon writing. In the background very low is the new Marianne Faithful LP which is a delightful way to create white noise while I scribble on the page. Hélène is home from her voice lesson, so the energy shifts as it does with different moments and thoughts. A good day a quiet day and it's delightfully ours. Be kind and find your quiet moments where you can. Peace.

January 13

Waiting for dinner to cook. Sipping a beer here at the computer and watching and listening to this... [Destroy All Monsters]

I have seen this band perform and it was astounding. When I think of the music I heard being born and raised in the Windsor and Detroit cities and area I say thank you because it was such a unique soundtrack for my youth in the 60's and 70's and 80's.
Cheers, enjoy.

January 12

Nothing to really express after a night behind the bar. After work in days gone by we would late night stop at Fran's restaurant and kibitz till 7am. Now, these days home and a well buttered piece of toast and a triple Jack and soda then to bed. Slowing down as time clicks off the moments and the years. Looking forward to a Bunker day tomorrow just family and some reading and writing. For sure some gawd awful tv and bad snacks mixed with red wine. Have a good one love all you can and change how you think about the things you can't love right now. Be kind always. Peace.

January 12

This glass of Pilsner beer touched with salt and married with tomato juice marks the end of the first part of my day. Been to the theatre and the bank to get change for the club night tonight. Did a bit of paperwork and walked over to Gay Loblaws with Hélène to get a chicken to roast for dinner tonight. Now I'm getting ready to roast the chicken drink the drink and after head out to bartend for 200 of my closest friends, who will be screaming and spinning to their favourite songs. Life is full life is full of wonder. Enjoy the fun and wonderment of others especially the young as though it was yours. Be kind and Peace.

January 11

Up early today although I feel as though I am down a couple of quarts of sleep time. Read and worked on some readings for the Jan 26th poetry marathon at Glad Day Books. Got my hair done and now I am in my reading chair eating my mushrooms on toast and drinking my coffee that Hélène made and served me on my favourite wooden tray. Getting ready to leave the bunker and experience the day. Being tired can push the experience either way but I find if I am tired and don't want the day to go to shit I have to be very mindful and focused. Not a bad thing it helps with the thought processes and creates a beautiful field of ideas to pick and look at and enjoy later when my energy returns. Find your perfect thought today and cherish it. Be kind. Peace.

January 10

This is Pirate, brother to his sister Pearl. He is here with all of us as I read my chosen books and Hélène does her crossword puzzle. She has a hot chocolate mixed with strawberry vodka and I am on my last Jack and soda. We had a day of doctors and emotion around realizing that all though we are certified in good health we have some physical issues associated with just being lucky enough to age. The ying and yang of being alive and living our lives as full as we are able to at any moment. We are happy and content to be here as a full family of two and four footers. Tomorrow office duties and my first day back to working out in over a month because of knee issues. It's good to be alive and for the moment everything seems easy and simple. We will take it. Be kind and Peace.

January 4

…Pearl, she is hanging with me as I wait for my white bean and barley soup to slowly draw into itself. We are listening to the Stones Beggars Banquet and I am sipping my before work bourbon and Guinness. The old lady is in the other room completely mind fucked by what's going on in US politics. The shit some people throw at their fellow humankind. Today it's the USA. Tomorrow it could be easily us. Never say never. All we can do is one small kindness at a time and keep each other safe. Peace.

January 2

Sipping a double Jack Daniels mixed with a touch of soda and topped up with champagne.

January 1

Watching almost 600 of my closest friends enjoy the fantastic talent on the big stage in the big room. The fun i have. Happy New Year to all the workers at Buddies and all those that support theatre and art and especially support what our theatre stands for. Be kind. Peace

December 31, 2018
Making black bean soup for tomorrow. Next year, remember not to touch your face eyes and your hmmmmm before you really thoroughly wash the jalapeño juice and guts off your hands. I may be fucking 64 years old but sometimes stupid invades a few of my moments. LOL. Happy New Year. Be kind tonight and all year and Peace.

December 31, 2018
It's going to be a great one. No poetry no bands no readings no high art. There will be two Dj's and dancing in the "big room" super talented queens cocktails sex (if the moment seizes you) 500 of your closest friends. Its not free but its cheap. See you there.

December 29, 2018

…our little jade Buddha that occupies the space in front of our remembrance candle which we try and light daily and at moments when those who we love and have moved on seem close. It doesn't matter what you believe or what your religion is. This is to remind us as we search for the human light to help us move through our day that it's so easy to forget the divine in us and around us. This thought brought to me something Lou Reed said, "Too much human and not enough divine." How true does that seem at times. Let's celebrate the divine within us and around us. Be kind and Peace.

December 27, 2018

Oh Christmas you were a great guest but summer wishing you were here now.

December 26, 2018

Watching my Christmas present from Hélène a Blu ray of the Stones in Hyde Park and all the while sipping a Guinness and a rebel yell bourbon after a lovely night of dear friends and too much food and wine. Merry Christmas.

December 24, 2018

Hélène is decorating a little bit for Christmas and I am loving her choices of decorations. Just pulled our dinner out of the oven at 11:30pm and letting it mellow under aluminum foil. Giving it time as I still have a shot and a beer to finish before we dine. Been a day, I have been to heaven and hell and back again a few times in less than 14 hours. Annie Lennox is singing Christmas to us from the stereo speakers. Right now everything fits and love has nudged its way in wearing a Santa hat. Be peaceful be kind struggle for the moments that are truly yours. Peace

December 21, 2018

Work tonight, I will be behind the bar dealing up the cocktails for another busy Friday club night. Resting up reading and sipping a vodka and limeade. Give yourself a little hug for making through another moment, day, and year. It's your journey so enjoy it when you can and learn from it when you can't. Be kind. Peace.

Afterword

A Hint of Perfection...

*And what rough beast, its hour come round at last,
Slouches towards Bethlehem to be born?*

Yeats

This is not a perfect book, but neither is my life nor will my life ever be perfect. I have lived my life chasing non-perfect things along with chasing gods, people, situations and things that I thought had a hint of perfection in or about them. There were so many dragons and beasts and needs that I chased only to realize that when I saw them clearly they where battered windmills spinning in the wind of reality. I now at this time in my life fully embrace my imperfections and realize the closest I can get to perfection is to love all that is imperfect in and around me. So this book reads as I read myself as a non-perfect person, and that makes me perfectly happy.

Patricia Wilson, April 2019

Patricia Wilson
Patricia was born on the same day Elvis Presley recorded and sparked the rock and roll era with "That's All Right Mama." Since then she has been chasing the roll wherever she can find it. Peace.

David Bateman (editor)
David Bateman was born on the same day that Elvis Presley recorded "Love Me Tender." Since then he has always wanted to be Ann-Margret in Viva Las Vegas.

photo by Adam Coish

Hélène Ducharme, Patricia Wilson and the four footers in the bunker

Made in the USA
Columbia, SC
28 December 2019